# To Ruin a Gentleman

## The Scarlet Chronicles: Book I

### Shana Galen

# Also by Shana Galen

REGENCY SPIES
*While You Were Spying*
*When Dashing Met Danger*
*Pride and Petticoats*

MISADVENTURES IN
MATRIMONY
*No Man's Bride*
*Good Groom Hunting*
*Blackthorne's Bride*
*The Pirate Takes a Bride*

SONS OF THE
REVOLUTION
*The Making of a Duchess*
*The Making of a Gentleman*
*The Rogue Pirate's Bride*

JEWELS OF THE TON
*If You Give a Duke a*
*Diamond*
*If You Give a Rake a Ruby*
*Sapphires are an Earl's*
*Best Friend*

LORD AND LADY SPY
*Lord and Lady Spy*
*The Spy Wore Blue*
*(novella)*
*True Spies*
*Love and Let Spy*
*All I Want for Christmas is*
*Blue (novella)*
*The Spy Beneath the*
*Mistletoe (novella)*

COVENT GARDEN CUBS
*Viscount of Vice (novella)*
*Earls Just Want to Have*
*Fun*
*The Rogue You Know*
*I Kissed a Rogue*

THE SURVIVORS
*Third Son's a Charm*
*No Earls Allowed*
*An Affair with a Spare*
*Unmask Me if You Can*

THE SCARLET
CHRONICLES
*To Ruin a Gentleman*
*Traitor in Her Arms*
*Taken by the Rake* (coming
February 2019)
*To Tempt a Rebel* (coming
March 2019)

STANDALONES AND
ANTHOLOGIES
*Mrs. Brodie's Academy for*
*Extraordinary Young Ladies*
*(duo)*
*Stealing the Duke's Heart*
*(duet)*
*The Summer of Wine and*
*Scandal (novella)*
*A Royal Christmas (duet)*
*The Dukes of Vauxhall*
*(anthology)*
*A Grosvernor Square*
*Christmas (anthology)*

## Dedication and Acknowledgements

This book is dedicated to Joanna Mackenzie who always believed in this series.

Special thanks to
 Joanna Mackenzie for editing,
 Kim Killion for the cover design,
 Martha Trachtenberg for copyediting,
 Monique Daoust for proofreading,
 and Abby Saul for formatting, uploading, and generally making everything come together.

# *One*

The Right Honorable Thomas Daventry, only son of the Viscount Daventry, hadn't been home in ages. It wasn't that he didn't get on with his parents. He did. It was more that he didn't get on with Hampshire. The rolling fields dotted with puffy white sheep were certainly bucolic, but they were also tedious as hell. At nineteen, what did Thomas want with sheep and fields and an old drafty pile? London with its artists and theaters and clubs was far more exciting than Daventry Hall.

Or was it?

After last night, Thomas wondered if perhaps the old pile and his staid father and mother had unplumbed depths. And if his father was keeping secrets, Thomas wanted to know.

Which was precisely why he'd ridden hell-for-leather the last few hours to reach home.

Just after noon the sun peeked out from behind low-hanging clouds that had threatened rain, and Thomas crested the rise overlooking the stately house. It had been built in the last century by some famous architect or another. Thomas considered the man an architect with little imagination. How difficult was it to design a gray stone rectangular building? Daventry Hall was all symmetry and proportion, right angles and clean lines. Not a column, not a tower, not a turret (whatever that was) to be seen. It was stable and predictable, like his parents.

Seeing the house again, Thomas almost turned right back around. It was foolishness coming here and confronting his parent about the information he'd received last night.

On the other hand, as long as he was here, he might as well have a meal.

Half an hour later, Thomas joined his father in the library. This dark-paneled room with plush couches and heavy draperies had always been his favorite room in the house, and he'd read most of the books it contained. Thomas had done his share of writing as well. He fancied himself a bit of a poet, though he'd yet to sell any of his verse.

Like the library, the viscount looked much as he always had, though his dark hair was mostly gray now, and he wore his spectacles more often than in the past. The viscount removed them now and gave Thomas a long look from behind the polished desk.

"What have you done now?"

Thomas scowled. "What's that supposed to mean? Can't I come for a visit?" He sat in one of the chairs across from the desk and admired the shelves of books.

The viscount tapped his fingers on the desk, while the low fire in the hearth crackled. "Have you gambled away your allowance?"

"No. Of course not."

"Fallen in love with an actress?"

"You'll need to increase my allowance if I'm to catch the eye of any actresses."

"Noted. What is it then? Been challenged to a duel? Lost your credit—"

"None of those. I haven't done anything except attend a dinner party."

The viscount steepled his hands. "Go on."

"I met an interesting gentleman there. A Sir Andrew Ffoulkes. He claims to know you."

Thomas had been watching his father's face, else he would not have noticed how all expression was wiped away. The viscount looked perfectly blank.

"Do you know him?" Thomas asked.

"No." His father's voice was level and without tone.

"That's funny. He…well, it's ludicrous really. I shouldn't have bothered you with it." He stood.

"What did this Ffoulkes say?"

Thomas shrugged. "He said to tell you hello and for me to ask you about the real Scarlet Pimpernel."

The viscount's fingers, steepled a moment before, now locked together. "The Scarlet Pimpernel."

"You know, the old story about the Englishman who rescued Frenchies during their revolution. Everyone says Sir Percy Blakeney was the pimpernel, but this Ffoulkes said to ask you about the real pimpernel."

The viscount rose and crossed to a small table with a crystal decanter. It wasn't dusty—nothing in the house was dusty—but Thomas had never seen his father drink from its contents before. Now, he poured himself two fingers of the amber liquid and drank it down before pouring another two.

Are quite you well?" Thomas asked, concern, and not a little excitement, beginning to grow. "Did you know the Scarlet Pimpernel? Was it Sir Percy?"

His father looked at him. "I suppose there's no point in keeping it hidden any longer."

Thomas sank back into his chair, his gaze fixed on his father. This was what he had come for, and yet, he couldn't quite believe his father had a story to tell. Viscount Daventry—Dull Daventry, as everyone called him in Town.

"I did know Ffoulkes," the viscount said. "It's habit to deny it, but the truth is I knew him well. I knew Blakeney too. I knew them all—Dewhurst, Hastings, the whole league." He sipped his drink. "And I suppose you are correct that Sir Percy was part of the League of the Scarlet Pimpernel."

"He wasn't the Scarlet Pimpernel?"

"He was *a* pimpernel, not *the* pimpernel."

"I'm not sure I follow. If he was not *the* pimpernel, who was?"

His father set his drink on the desk and gave Thomas a hard look.

"Are you saying?" Thomas shook his head. It was not possible. His father could not be the Scarlet Pimpernel. "I-I cannot believe it."

\*\*\*

Hugh could hardly fault his son for the look of pure incredulity that crossed his face. It wasn't every day a child's parent admitted to being England's most celebrated hero. Hugh had never wanted acclaim or recognition. That's why he'd given it to Blakeney, but he couldn't start there. If he was to tell his son the tale, he should start at the beginning. But what exactly was the beginning?

Even as he thought it, the remembered scent of fresh apples and cut hay and sweet clover seemed to infuse the room. Because, of course, it all began in Versailles, and it all began with her.

# *Two*

*Versailles 1789*

Angelette enjoyed dining alone. She'd risen early so she might have some solitude before her guests joined her, which meant she was not pleased when her butler announced the arrival of a Viscount Daventry.

With a pained expression, she'd dabbed at her mouth. "Show him in."

The English had no manners. Not only was the man a full two days late to the house party, he had the gall to arrive at the ungodly hour of half past seven. She never should have invited him. She'd only done so because her sister had written to her and begged a favor.

Thérèse was in London and had met and befriended the viscount, who was apparently an avid importer of French wines. When he'd said he was traveling to France on business, Thérèse had invited him to stay with her and her husband, the Marquis de Beauvais, at their château and vineyard. Thérèse hoped the viscount would consider importing the de Beauvais family wines to England. But Thérèse had written to say the marquis's business in England had taken longer than expected. Would dear Angelette extend the viscount an invitation to her house party? Angelette had done so, and now the man himself had deigned to make an appearance.

His footsteps echoed on the marble floor as he followed the butler to the dining room. The door opened and she rose, smoothing her pale pink skirts. After wearing black for so long, it still seemed strange to look down and see color. But she was not in mourning any longer.

"Madame, Lord Daventry."

She looked up and into the handsome face of the man standing in her dining room entry. He sported wavy brown hair, which was bare of both a wig or powder and which he'd pulled into a short queue and fastened with a plain black thong. No ribbon of silk for him. His eyes were blue, not dark blue like hers but the clear, bright blue of the cornflowers that dotted the fields near the château in the spring. He was neither plain nor too handsome, his face oval with prominent cheekbones and a straight nose. He looked fit and trim in his coat and waistcoat the color of champagne. His breeches fit snugly, showing his muscled calves to advantage.

He bowed when he entered, his eyes never leaving hers and his mouth lifting in a mischievous smile that made her breath catch in her chest.

No, she definitely should not have invited him.

"*Bonjour,* Madame la Comtesse."

"Good morning, Lord Daventry." With a nod, she dismissed the butler. "Won't you join me for breakfast, my lord?"

"English!" He took the chair a footman pulled out directly across from her. "It's music to my ears."

She lifted her cup. "Most people find French the more melodic of the two languages."

"I find French the more annoying of the two languages." He nodded to the footman who approached with a cup. "I don't suppose you have tea. *Une tasse de thé?*"

"*Oui, monsieur.*" The servant stepped away to prepare it.

"It's been an age since I heard English or drank tea."

"You are not much of a traveler, I suppose," she said, sipping her coffee.

"I do a fair amount of traveling, but I like my little pieces of civilization."

She raised her brows, amused despite herself. "And coffee is not civilized."

"It's a bitter and foul brew, and those who drink it have personalities to match."

She lifted her cup and sipped.

"What are you drinking?"

"The bitter and foul brew."

He laughed. "I've only just arrived and have already managed to insult you. You must forgive me. I haven't slept in three days."

"Is that why you've arrived two days late to the house party?"

His expression turned serious. "No. In fact, I wasn't certain I would arrive at all. I came through Paris."

"But Versailles is only a few hours' journey from Paris."

"The difficulty, Comtesse, was leaving Paris. Have you not heard?"

She shook her head. Since her husband's death, she'd paid little attention to French politics, eschewing the balls and court affairs at the Palace of Versailles as well as the theaters and galleries of Paris. She'd come to her late husband's Versailles estate because it was cooler in the summer than the château in Avignon. Not to mention, her brother-in-law was in Avignon now, as was his right, and he'd recently married and she thought it only polite to give him and his new wife privacy. Her mother, being English, had returned home when Angelette's father had died, but Angelette had friends in France, the closest being her older sister Thérèse, who was now the Marquise de Beauvais.

"I'm afraid I have not."

The viscount's gaze shifted to the footman, then back to her. "There are riots in Paris and mobs in the streets. The gates were closed for at least a day while the royal army attempted to restore order."

"The bread shortages," she said, understanding now. Years of poor crop yields had meant shortages of flour as well as other goods. She'd had to allot more money from her budget to buy the necessities, and she could only imagine what that meant for those without means. "No doubt the king and his ministers will find a solution."

Daventry glanced at the footman again. "If by that you mean locking the Third Estate out of the hall at Versailles and causing them to make pledges on a *jeu de paume*—you see how annoying that is? Three words when two, *tennis court,* would do. In any case, if panicking the commoners into taking oaths against their monarch on a tennis court is your king's policy, then I am less than impressed. The situation has gone from bad to worse."

Angelette gave her footman a pointed look. "Leave us," she said in French. She'd been speaking to the viscount in English, but she could not be certain the servants did not understand that language. The liveried footman left the room, closing the door behind him. When they were alone, she rose and walked around the table so she could speak softly.

The viscount rose when she did, meaning she had to look up at him when she stood before him. She had not considered that eventuality. She was not a short woman or particularly petite, but he made her feel both. "My lord—"

"Call me Daventry. Everyone does."

"Very well, Daventry. I do appreciate you making me aware of the situation in Paris, but you must understand this sort of discussion is most distasteful to the members of the nobility. I hope you will keep this news to yourself for the remainder of the house party."

His expression remained unchanged. "You want me to keep my mouth shut so you might bury your heads in the proverbial sand?"

"That's not what I'm saying—"

"Oh, I understand what you are saying, Comtesse. I don't think you understand what I am saying."

She folded her arms across her chest. "Which is?"

He bent down, leaning close to her. "You, and all the rest of your class, are in danger."

"Ridiculous. There have been excesses, of course. I understand the anger the lower classes feel, but neither I nor my late husband have treated our tenants unfairly. Not to mention, I am only half French and spent much of my youth in England."

"The mobs in Paris weren't asking those they confronted their nationality. If a lady or gentleman looked like a noble, he or she was a target."

"Of violence?"

"Not yet, but I have no doubt it is coming."

"And what do you suggest? Leave my home, my friends, my family?"

"You have family in England. I met both your mother and sister, and they asked me repeatedly to persuade you to return with me to England."

Angelette waved a hand. "The British papers exaggerate the unrest here and my sister is unnecessarily worried."

He gave her a long look. The intensity of his striking blue eyes made her shiver. "Madame, as I said, I have just come from Paris. I assure you the unrest is no exaggeration." He raised a hand before she could demur again. "I am heading for Calais and a packet to Dover tomorrow morning. I would like you to travel with me. I cannot force you, but if you choose to stay here, then I doubt we will meet again. Ever." He gave her a short bow. "Excuse me. Your butler offered to show me to my room." He marched out of the room, leaving her alone.

"What an annoying man," she muttered to herself. Thank God he'd be gone tomorrow morning.

\*\*\*

*Little angel, indeed,* Hugh thought that afternoon as he waited for his turn with bow and arrow. He'd never met a person so misnamed. She should have been named *little devil*. Unfortunately, he couldn't quite work out the French for that. He watched the comtesse raise her bow and narrow her eyes along the shaft of the arrow at the painted hay target. He had to admit, she looked angelic enough. Her dark curly hair had been arranged in an artful style and swept back and up. Her straw Bergère hat, worn on the crown of her head and tilted down over her forehead, was adorned with pink silk ribbon and an assortment of pink and white silk flowers. Tendrils of her dark hair spiraled down about her neck and blew across her pale cheek when the breeze rustled the trees. He couldn't help but notice that in the dappled sunlight her dark hair seemed to be infused with strands of red and gold.

Her *robe à l'anglaise* was pink silk with a white underskirt. It was far less ornate than what many of the other ladies wore, being devoid of ribbons and lace and other fripperies. He had heard some of the female guests remarking that the comtesse was only recently out of her widow's weeds. Hugh was of the opinion black would have suited her, since it was the color of Satan. The pink only made her look sweet and pretty. Hugh considered her neither.

The comtesse released her arrow and it flew straight and true, hitting the hay target just to the left of the center.

Everyone clapped politely. Everyone but Hugh. His turn was next, and he moved past the brightly clad French nobles to take the comtesse's place. A servant moved to collect her arrow from the target, but Hugh called, "Leave it."

The comtesse, who had been speaking to some duchesse or other, turned to give him her attention. "Won't my arrow be in your way, Monsieur le Vicomte?"

"No, madame. Not at all." He nocked his arrow and raised it. He hadn't planned to join in the activities at the house party. He'd wanted to bathe, change, and rest before departing for Calais. But his valet, who had been traveling with him, had informed him he could not possibly reach Calais in time to board the last packet to England. He might stay overnight and be on the first in the morning, but that would require saddling the horses and repacking and thus a very late arrival and inferior accommodations. Hugh's man suggested spending a comfortable night at the château of the Comtesse d'Avignon and leaving at first light.

Hugh reluctantly agreed, not just because staying at the château made more sense but because he had promised the Marquise de Beauvais he would do all in his power to bring her sister out of France. Hugh had bathed, eaten, and attempted to nap, but he could not sleep. Too restless to read, he'd joined the house party on the lawn for croquet and now archery. He supposed a boating party was next, as it appeared the servants were readying rowboats near a large pond just past the lawn.

After the tumult of Paris, Hugh felt as though he'd stepped into another world. No one but him was in any way concerned about the unrest in Paris. No one else seemed to hear the ticking clock, counting down the hours, perhaps minutes, until the bomb exploded. These pampered men and women really did not seem to realize they were in mortal danger, and every time he brought the issue up, someone made a witty rejoinder and the conversation moved on. But he hadn't given up on the comtesse yet. He still had the rest of the day and the evening to convince her to leave with him.

Hugh looked down the straight shaft and loosed the arrow. It flew true, landing just to the right of the not-so-angelic comtesse's arrow and perfectly in the center of the target.

The polite applause was subdued as was the comtesse's tone. "Well done, monsieur." She looked at the other guests and smiled brightly. "Shall we partake of refreshments?"

Hugh blew out a breath. It seemed the fairy tale continued.

She led them toward the tables nearby, set with china and silver and attended by liveried footmen in wigs. As Hugh started away, the duchesse his hostess had been speaking to earlier put her arm through his and walked beside him. She was blond and unremarkable except for the enormous ostrich plumes on her hat and the large jewels on her ears, throat, and fingers. She was in her mid-thirties, so comparable in age to himself.

"I hear you have just come from Paris, Monsieur le Vicomte."

"Please call me Daventry," he said.

She made a sound in her throat that seemed to sum up what she thought of this and of all English in particular. "Daventry, then. And tell me, how was Paris? My husband has business interests there and his managers report work is at a standstill."

"I can well believe it, madame. Travel in and out has been restricted, and when I was there, riots broke out on the streets."

She put a hand to her jeweled chest. "Goodness. Riots? Whatever for?"

Hugh steeled himself and called on his last reserves of patience. "As I understand it, the people of France are starving."

"Well, then they should cease rioting and go back to work. No wonder they are hungry."

They had reached the refreshment tables, laden with all sorts of delicacies. The men and women took plates with small cakes and tarts, nibbling them sparingly while sipping sparkling wine. In the house, a string quartet began to play, the lovely strains of Mozart wafting over the perfectly manicured lawns. It was not difficult to see why the duchesse did not understand the realities of life for the poor in the Faubourg of Saint-Antoine.

Hugh refused a plate, but accepted a glass of wine, drinking it down quickly.

"I shall tell the duc to replace those managers with others. Laziness among the lower classes cannot be tolerated."

A few of the other guests glanced at the duchesse, but conversation continued.

"I would urge you not to take such measures, madame. If the workers stay home, it is because the streets are not safe. The men and women your husband employs have families as well, and they must feel compelled to stay home and protect those they love."

"Good lord. You sound like that American ambassador. What is his name?"

"Jefferson."

"Yes. He goes on and on about equality. Quite tedious, really."

"I assure you I am no revolutionary. I lost a brother and a cousin in the American war. But even if talk of equality is tedious, surely compassion is always a welcome topic."

"Compassion! Those peasants reproduce like rabbits. Surely losing a few to hunger or disease will ease the strain on the country's resources and be better for all of us." She bit into a frosted morsel of cake.

"If that is how you really feel, then I suppose you deserve what is coming."

She arched a brow. "And what is that?"

He opened his mouth to answer, but the comtesse was immediately at his side. "Daventry, would you accompany me in the boat? I need a strong man to row." She smiled up at him, but her deep blue eyes were icy.

"Of course, Comtesse."

She drew him away from the others, steering him toward the pond. She smelled faintly of apples and champagne, and he placed his own hand over hers, feeling the heat of her skin through their gloves.

"My lord, I thought we had agreed at breakfast that no more should be said on the topic of Paris." She said this lightly, but her eyes were fierce.

"I don't recall agreeing to that. In fact, to do so would be irresponsible. Your friends should be apprised of the situation. They would do well to protect themselves and their families."

Her hand on his forearm tightened, and he looked down at her slim fingers encased in white gloves. "My friends do not want to be warned. They want to have an enjoyable outing, and as this is my first house party since my husband's death, I ask that you not ruin it with your dire pronouncements."

Hugh stopped and turned to look directly into her face. His mouth went slightly dry at the fierceness of her expression. She had strength and courage, misplaced as it was. "Comtesse, I know you have been in mourning. You have been in seclusion. Perhaps you do not fully understand the situation in your adopted country. You and the rest of your class are in danger. I cannot say it more clearly. Your sister and mother are in London. They wish you to join them. Why not go to them until this unrest quiets?"

She shook her head. "I may be part English, but I am also part French. My husband was French. I have land and responsibilities here. It is my country, and I will not flee like a puppy with her tail between her legs. The king and the Palace of Versailles are less than a mile away. I assure you, we are quite safe here."

She wasn't safe, and he didn't know what more he could do to sway her opinion. He would have liked to pick her up, toss her over his shoulder, and carry her away. But as enjoyable as that would be, he was supposed to be a civilized man, and she was an independent woman.

"Then you will not come with me to Calais in the morning?" he asked.

"No. I will stay here and defend what is mine and my family's."

He changed direction, pulling her into the shade of a tree and thus out of the view of the other guests. She stepped away from him, her back to the tree trunk. Hugh leaned close to her, boxing her in. It was the sort of thing he wouldn't normally do to a woman, but she left him little choice. "And how do you think to defend yourself?" The scent of apples and pine tickled his nose, making him even more aware of her. "Do you suppose your servants are loyal to you? You are afraid to speak freely in front of them. Do you have an army hiding somewhere we cannot see? When the mobs of Paris march on the palace and Versailles, how will you defend yourself?"

"It will never come to that, monsieur. The unrest in Paris will be put down, and all will be well." She gave him a small shove backward and gestured toward the lake. "Now, which boat shall we take?"

Hugh took her hand in his and lifted it to his mouth. He paused, lips brushing over her glove, his eyes meeting hers. Her breath hitched slightly, and he watched her throat work as she swallowed. "Forgive me," he murmured. "I've had enough of rowing in circles for one day. Excuse me."

He dropped her hand and took long strides back toward the château.

# *Three*

Angelette had hoped not to see Daventry again. She'd hoped he would stay confined to his chamber until such time as he could arrange transport to Calais. She was not so fortunate. First, he attended dinner, where he insisted on discussing what he'd seen in Paris with the Marquis de Caritat. Angelette had managed to steer the conversation away, but she was growing quite weary of the viscount's dire prophecies. She was not fully able to control the conversation, however, as she was distracted by her staff. She had instructed her butler she wanted one footman to serve each guest at dinner. Instead, several guests had to share a footman and thus had to wait at times for their requests to be granted.

Between dinner and the ball, she'd had to change hastily into her scarlet ball gown as the butler requested a moment of her time to tell her several of the male servants had become ill and had taken to their beds. It was all quite strange as everyone had seemed perfectly well earlier in the day.

And then the string quartet had been a trio. The cellist had gone home to see to an emergency. Angelette found herself in the position of having to apologize to her guests yet again. The house party was to go on two more days, and she could only hope this would be the last of the inconveniences. Still, after all of Daventry's dire predictions, she couldn't help feel that the servants' absences felt suspicious. Was she blind to what was really happening?

It didn't help that she'd been distracted by thoughts of the viscount all afternoon. How had he managed to make a kiss on the hand—her *gloved* hand—so erotic? For the first time in months and months she'd felt the heat of attraction and arousal. She'd tried to convince herself it was because he was a novelty, someone new among the same group of powdered and stuffed men she usually surrounded herself with.

But she feared there was more to her attraction than just a fresh male face...and figure.

She was drawn back to the ball when her first dance partner, the Duc de Limousin, claimed his dance. He was graceful, if not clever, which meant she did not have to worry about her toes but did have to work hard at making conversation. As he led her through the forms of the minuet, she could not help but watch Daventry lead the Duchesse de Limousin in the same steps. He was not graceful nor did his attire draw the eye. In fact, in his black and silver silk coat, silver waistcoat, and black breeches, he looked positively funereal. With his broad shoulders and imposing height, he seemed to take up much more of the large ballroom than he ought. By right, she should have been the center of attention, but it was clear most of the onlookers watched him. Angelette could hardly fault them when she did it too. She couldn't stop herself from studying the way his hand touched the duchess's and remembering the way he'd held her hand, pressed his lips to her glove. She could imagine him peeling that glove off and pressing a kiss to her palm, her wrist, sliding his tongue up her inner arm…

"Are you feeling quite well?" the duc asked. "Your cheeks are flushed."

She dragged her gaze from the viscount. "I can't think why." Her voice was breathless. "I suppose it's because I haven't danced in so long."

"You must miss your late husband terribly," he said, his painted lips turning down in sympathy.

"I do." Perhaps that was the problem. She had loved Georges when she wed him and continued to love him for the two years they had been married. He was a good man, kind and pleasant. In the eighteen months since he'd died of a fever, she had missed his companionship. Perhaps if they'd had a child together, she might not have been so lonely, but though they'd tried, she had failed to conceive.

Now, looking at Daventry, she accepted another reason she missed her husband. She would go to bed alone tonight. For the first time since Georges had died, her body ached for the touch of a man. She wanted to be held, to be kissed, to be caressed in the dark. She couldn't say why Daventry should arouse these emotions in her. She did not like the man...and yet her gaze strayed again to his hands and she imagined them once again on her bare skin.

A crash sounded and she glanced toward the doors to the ballroom. The servants were supposed to be bringing in refreshments for later. They had undoubtedly dropped something. She hoped her guests would be forgiving, as it was her first ball out of mourning. Just as she began to give some excuse to the duc, she heard shouting and another crash.

The musicians ceased playing and her guests began to murmur.

"Excuse me," she said. "I shall see what the matter is. Please, continue dancing—"

The door to the ballroom burst open and a barefoot man dressed in a dirty white shirt and trousers stumbled inside. For a moment he appeared stunned at what he saw, but when the nearest footman challenged him, he raised the shovel he carried and struck.

Angelette screamed. The duc shoved her behind him, but she could still see the rise and fall of the shovel.

Several of the male guests started toward the peasant, but when more peasants rushed in after him, brandishing shovels and picks, her guests skidded to a stop. Shouts of "What is this about?" and "Get out!" and "Put down your weapons" resounded. Angelette knew she should do something. This was her château. She had to stop this. She pushed away from the duc, coming forward, only to have her arm seized violently and her entire body wrenched away.

She stumbled back, colliding with Daventry. "Come with me," he said, pulling her whether she wanted to go or not.

"But you are taking me in the wrong direction."

He was dragging her toward the French doors that opened into the garden. "I'm trying to help you escape."

"But I have to see—"

A woman screamed and Angelette looked back to see more peasants had entered.

"You can thank me for saving your life later. Now, run!" He pulled her, and she was forced to follow him, whether she wanted to go or not. Another scream pierced the room, and Angelette stopped resisting. Lifting her skirts, she ran beside Daventry. Together they flung open the doors and ran onto the terrace. Light spilled from the ballroom onto the paving stones, but beyond was darkness.

"Which way to the stable?" Daventry asked.

"That way." She pointed.

"We'll ride to the palace and request assistance."

"Yes." The king's guards would come and take the attackers into custody. She might not like Daventry, but she could acknowledge he was no fool. She followed him into the shadows, down the steps, and along the path toward the stable. Behind her came the shouts of men, the clang of metal on metal, and the screams of women. She shivered, though the summer evening was warm.

"You couldn't do anything to help," Daventry said as though reading her thoughts. "If you were still there, you would be dead too."

Bile rose in her throat as she realized everything Daventry had tried to warn her about was true. The pieces fell into place; the missing servants, the sick footmen, the rumors. Then she thought of her friends lying dead or injured in her ballroom. She should not have abandoned them. This was her home. She had invited her friends, and she felt responsible for their safety. They needed to summon the palace guards as quickly as possible.

Daventry had released her hand, but now as they neared the edge of the house, he grasped her wrist. "Stay close."

"You think there are more of them outside?"

"I don't know what to think."

Angelette's heart beat fast as they moved into the open area between the house and the stable. It was still early evening and the moon had not yet risen high enough in the sky to give any light. She knew her way well enough, but the slippers she wore were not made for walking on the gravel path. Sharp stones stabbed the soles of her feet and she moved carefully, wincing every few steps.

"That's it," she said when the stable came into view. Light flickered in one of the windows, making the stable look welcoming. She had a spare pair of riding boots inside, and she could change into those before starting for Versailles. Normally, she would have balked at the prospect of arriving at the palace in old riding boots and a ball gown, but fashion didn't seem to matter any longer. She rushed ahead of Daventry, eager to reach the light and the safety of the stable.

"Madame, wait!" he called.

She turned to look over her shoulder, to assure him she was fine, and when she looked back it was just in time to avoid colliding with the man who had stepped into the path. Angelette screamed as he raised something long and metallic-looking. She ducked quickly, feeling the whoosh of air past her ear as the weapon just missed colliding with her head. A jagged stone dug into her foot, but she ignored the pain and focused on righting herself. If she stumbled and fell, she would be dead. She moved to the side with little grace but managed to stay on her feet and to back up and out of the attacker's reach.

"One of them is trying to escape!" the attacker called in French.

"Get out of the way," Daventry ordered. The attacker brandished what looked like a poker at the viscount.

"Make me, English scum."

With growing horror, Angelette realized the man blocking their path to the stables was no peasant. He wore her blue and gold livery. In fact, she knew him to be one of her footmen.

"Exactly what do you think you are doing?" she demanded. "Get out of my way."

He sneered at her. "I don't answer to you anymore, Angelette."

She didn't know what shocked her more. His insolent tone or the fact that he dared use her Christian name.

"All men are equal, and I'll kill every last one of you aristos if that's what it takes."

"You're mad," she whispered. She gave the stable a fleeting look, and the footman struck again. This time she would have been hit, but Daventry moved quickly, grasping the attacker's arm and wrenching it back up.

"Go!" he told Angelette.

She didn't hesitate. She lifted her skirts and ran for the stables. The doors were standing open, and she rushed inside. The lantern hanging nearby was lit, and she glanced about for some sort of weapon. She spotted several tools for mucking out the stalls, but they were too heavy and cumbersome for her to wield. Instead, she grasped the hoof knife the farrier used and slid it into the hidden pocket under her skirts. She lifted the lantern from its nail and held it up, searching for her boots when footsteps behind her caused her to swing around.

The light from the lantern illuminated Daventry. His look was dark and serious and a red stain bloomed on his white shirt. She gasped, but he waved a hand. "It's not mine."

She closed her eyes, not wanting to think of the footman and his fate. What was happening? In the space of a half hour, the entire world had turned on its side. She felt dizzy and confused, sure of only one thing: she must reach Versailles and the king.

Daventry cocked his head, his brows lowering. Angelette started to ask what the matter was, and then she noticed it too. The stables were too quiet. She should have heard the snorting of the horses, the sound of their hooves pawing the ground, the creak of the floorboards as they moved in their stalls. She heard nothing.

"No!" Surely the peasants would not have harmed the horses. She rushed down the length of the stable. Stall after stall she passed was empty. She ran the entire length, then spun around. "I don't understand."

"They didn't want anyone escaping and turned the horses loose."

Angelette straightened her shoulders. "Then we walk to Versailles. It's not far."

He gave her a dubious look. "We'll have to stay off the roads. How do you intend to walk through brush and woods in your slippers and silk gown?"

"You don't know me very well, my lord, if you think that will stop me." She ran back to the stable door. "Keep watch while I find boots and do something about my dress."

He moved to the stable door and peered into the night. All was quiet for the moment, but she knew it wouldn't last. She found her boots and sat to remove her slippers before slipping the boots on. Next she stood and looked down at her dress. She had limited movement in the wide panniers. Without them, the skirt would drag on the ground. She would have to remove the skirt and panniers and go in her petticoats and shift. As the bodice was a separate piece, she could keep it on. She reached back to untie her skirts and could not seem to loosen the knot. She began to unpin the skirt so she could slide it around and see what she was doing when Daventry moved closer.

"Would you like my help?"

She did not want his help, but she was also smart enough to realize that if it hadn't been for him, she would probably be dead by now. She was fortunate he had taken her with him when he'd escaped the ballroom. Her hesitation then might have been the cause of their deaths. And she would not be the one to hamper their escape now.

"Thank you." She gave him her back and felt his hands on her waist. She struggled to stop her thoughts from returning to their earlier path. Struggled not to imagine his hands on her bare skin. Instead, she took a deep breath and tried to pretend it was her lady's maid loosening her ties and sliding the heavy skirts over her panniers and down her legs. "Now the panniers, if you don't mind."

"Of course."

Was it her imagination or was his voice huskier than usual?

It seemed to take an eternity before he finally undid the knot and freed her from the panniers. He slid them down, brushing his hand along the small of her back.

"Forgive me," he said hastily, jerking his hand back.

Angelette swallowed. "It's nothing."

But it hadn't been nothing. His touch seemed to burn through the thin layers of muslin that comprised her undergarments. Even though she could not feel his skin on hers, heat flashed through her, traveling straight to her lower abdomen where it settled and pulsed. The sensation made her legs weak, but she managed to step away from him and finish removing the panniers herself.

She gathered the garments from the floor, looking about for a hook to hang them so the material would not be soiled.

"Leave it," Daventry said.

But she needed something to do, something to take her mind off the heat pulsing through her. "This gown is new, and I'd rather—"

"Leave it!"

His voice erased any warmth remaining. She swung around to stare at him, but he wasn't looking at her. He was staring out of the stable at the twinkling stars that had appeared.

"What is it?" But he didn't need to answer because she saw. The twinkling lights she'd thought were stars weren't stars at all but...torches. And the people carrying those torches were nearing, coming closer.

"Mon Dieu," she whispered.

"Yes." He turned to her. "I was afraid of this."

"What is that?"

"More peasants are coming to burn the château."

"No." She shook her head. She couldn't believe they would burn her home. "I don't understand. The villagers here have always been treated well. Most serve at the palace or in the households of the courtiers—"

"I don't think those are the villagers from Versailles. I think those are men and women from Paris. They must have come and turned your servants against you. Now they're here to burn the symbols of the upper classes to the ground."

"But we can't let them. This château has stood for hundreds of years. The art inside is priceless. We have to stop them!"

"We have to run or we'll both be murdered."

She wanted to argue. She'd never felt so completely impotent in her life. This was her home. This had been her husband's home. Almost all of her worldly possessions were inside—keepsakes and mementos she cherished. She could never replace the lock of hair Georges had given her or the drawing her sister had made of their baby brother who had died in infancy. But all of these items were merely things. They weren't worth her life.

"We go out the back," he said.

She didn't argue. She followed him through the empty stable and out the back door. As he stepped out, she noted he'd donned a spare pair of riding boots, leaving his dancing shoes in their place. Behind the stable lay the paddocks and a wooded area where she often rode.

"We'll head for the safety of the woods and the cover of the trees," he said.

"But the palace is that way."

"And so are the peasants with their torches. We'll have to make a wide flank around them and proceed with caution, as we can't be certain they haven't also attacked the palace."

The words *don't be ridiculous* were on the tip of her tongue, but she didn't speak them. Nothing was too outrageous to be believed. Not after what she'd seen tonight.

"I suppose there's but one way to find out."

He nodded. "Stay close."

She glanced at the dark woods and needed no further encouragement. She threaded her fingers through his and followed him into the unknown.

# *Four*

Her hand trembled in his. Hugh could hardly blame her. He'd known immediately what was happening. His first inclination had been similar to that of many of the other men—fight. The peasants were thin and armed with household tools. He could have overpowered them.

But his thoughts had turned to the Comtesse d'Avignon and his commitment to her sister. He couldn't fight the peasants and protect her. The other women were married and had husbands to defend them, but she had no one. She'd worn a stunning red gown tonight, and it was simple to spot her in the ballroom. If his eyes were drawn to her, then the assailants' eyes would be as well. She was very much like the center of the target they'd hit in their game of archery that morning.

He'd taken three long strides and grasped her hand, pulling her out of harm's way. Now it seemed he was in a similar position, leading her once again away from the danger. She trudged along beside him without complaint, keeping up, though it must have been hard for her at the punishing pace he set. Once they were under the cover of the trees, he turned and looked back at the château. The men and women with torches had reached it, and the flickering firelight seemed to dance around it. Hugh did not want to stay to see it burn. He prayed to God some of the others had escaped. He had not particularly liked any of them, but they didn't deserve to be bludgeoned or burned to death.

"You needn't stop because of me. I'm fine," she said, though she was panting. No doubt her corset was tightly laced and prevented her from taking a deep breath. He made the mistake of glancing at her bodice and his gaze focused on the plump half-moons of her breasts rising and falling from the scarlet material. He immediately looked down and then frowned.

"Your petticoats are too bright. They'll be a beacon for anyone searching for us."

She looked down as well, then back up. "Your coat is no better. The silver reflects."

She was right. "I'll turn it inside out." He pulled it off, while she bent and scooped up earth. "What are you doing?"

"Making certain my petticoats aren't so white."

She was a smart girl and not so missish she objected to a little dirt. He'd known women who would rather die than suffer a stain on their dresses. He would have still helped her if she'd been such a woman, but she would not have endeared herself to him. He didn't particularly want to feel warmly toward Angelette, but he'd been drawn to her from the first and it seemed fate—with a little help from Hugh— had thrown them together.

When Hugh had turned both coat and waistcoat inside out so their silver embroidery was muted, he glanced at Angelette. She had mud smeared over her petticoats and was using them, without much success, to try and clean her hands. She looked up at him, and he had to suppress a smile. She had a smear of mud across her cheek, which made her look like a wayward child who had been playing where she oughtn't.

"That's much better," she said, nodding her approval of him. "How do I look?"

"Very well. It's just—" He gestured to her face.

"I have mud on my face?"

"Your cheek."

She swiped at the wrong cheek, smudging it with mud.

"No. Now you've made it worse."

She rubbed at the mud she'd added, smearing it further.

He grasped her hand. "Allow me." Withdrawing his handkerchief, he gently cleaned the mud from one cheek and then the other. She stood very still, her gaze focused on the vicinity of his ear. When he withdrew his hand, her gaze met his.

"Better?"

It was difficult to see, and without thinking, he took her chin between two fingers and angled her head. Her quickly indrawn breath was a stark reminder that he shouldn't have touched her so intimately. To do so with a handkerchief out of necessity was one thing, but with his bare hand was another.

And yet, he didn't pull his hand away. Her skin was soft and warm, her chin sharp and pointed—the perfect tip to her heart-shaped face. He had the mad urge to slide his fingers up and over the newly cleaned skin of her cheek and test its softness.

She stiffened and he wondered if she'd read his thoughts, but one look at her eyes told him that was not the reason. Releasing her, he followed her gaze. The château had begun to burn, the flames spiking high into the black night. Screams echoed, but from this distance it was impossible to tell whether they were screams of delight or pain.

He tried to think of something comforting to say, but there was nothing. It was hard not to see the peasants' point of view. For so long they had suffered unfairly under a rule that favored the wealthy and powerful. Was it not right that they fought for some measure of equality? And yet, as a member of the nobility himself, he could not imagine seeing his ancestral home burned to the ground. He might have been given his title, but with it came great responsibility and the care of land and tenants and everything else that came with running a great estate. He had spent years learning how to manage Daventry Hall and years ensuring that its lands were profitable and his tenants and servants well taken care of. Not every landowner was so responsible, but did one throw out an entire harvest because of a few rotten apples?

Tears glittered on the comtesse's cheeks, and he took her hand, squeezing it. "Let's go. I don't know what other mischief is planned for the night, but the sooner we reach the palace, the better."

She nodded, turning her face away from the fiery inferno of her home with a resolute look. "Only the king can help us now, and I don't hold out much hope he will be of any use."

Hugh took her hand, surprised at how icy cold it was even in the warm night. Since they could not take the most direct path to Versailles lest they encounter a mob of peasants, they would have to travel farther into the woods before cutting back. He started toward the deeper section of woods, where the trees grew thick, keeping her at his side.

"I have not ever met the French king," he said, "but I understand the mantle of power does not fit him."

"He would much rather hunt or repair clocks than deal with matters of state. It's not that he is unintelligent."

"Watch your step here."

"I see it. Thank you." She had to lift her petticoat to climb over a fallen log. "But he is perhaps too introspective. It is not easy for him to make decisions, and these times call for decisive action."

"And the queen?"

"She is the stronger of the two. Wait." She bent and yanked at her skirts. "I'm caught." She struggled further until finally managing to free herself, but not until he heard the rip of muslin. "There." She took his hand again, and he was pleased at the gesture. He could at least provide her some compassion, some comfort through his touch.

"What was I saying?"

"You were telling me about the queen." He led her deeper into the woods, beginning now to look for a place to cut over. If only he had some light, he could move more quickly. As it was, they had to go slowly for fear of stumbling or tripping.

"She is clever and decisive. If she were in charge, I have no doubt these uprisings would have been put down long ago. But she is hampered by the people's dislike of her and her birth. Even after all these years, she's still considered Austrian. If the populace thought she influenced the king's decisions, he would lose what little popularity he has."

Which meant all their efforts to reach Versailles might be for naught. But he would not say so aloud. She had already lost everything. He could not take away her one last glimmer of hope.

They walked in silence for a long time, stopping occasionally so she might disentangle herself or he might help her over a piece of difficult ground.

"Should we not start toward Versailles now? I think we've gone far enough into the woods."

"I've already started that way. I'm looking for the road now. If it's clear, we can take it to the palace."

She stopped. "We're still walking away from the road. We have to turn that way to reach the palace." She pointed back the way they'd come.

"No, we've already been that way."

She withdrew her hand from his. "I know these woods, and I say we must go that way."

"You might know the woods near your château in the daylight, but it's dark and you're miles from home. Look at the stars." With all the branches above them, the stars were difficult to see. She moved to study them.

"I followed that one there and then turned east to follow that one." He frowned. Or had he been following that other one?

"Look how light the sky has become. It will be morning in a few hours."

He heard the weariness and frustration in her voice. Hugh did not think he was lost, but he could not be certain. His own instinct was to push on and make every attempt to reach the palace. But if he was walking in circles, he could hardly drag her along with him. She needed rest and surely they would make better progress in the daylight. It would be dangerous traveling in the light of day, but it was dangerous tromping through the woods in the dark when a misstep could cause a broken neck or leg.

"We should stop for a few hours." He explained his reasoning, and she agreed without protest. Before he could suggest finding a place to rest, she sank down onto the carpet of soil and leaves.

"I don't want to take another step," she said, lying on her back. "I would crawl for some water, but otherwise I simply want to lie here and not move."

Hugh might have preferred to find a more comfortable spot, perhaps one with a fallen log to sit on or somewhere near a small creek, but he too was weary. He lay down beside her and looked up at the sky. It was more gray than black now. Propping his hands behind his head, he studied it for a long time.

"Why did you help me?" she asked. She'd been silent for so long, he thought she'd fallen asleep.

"You were standing near me. It seemed natural."

She turned to look at him, and he could see her pale face in the dim light. "You were dancing with the duchesse. It would have been more natural to help her. She was much closer."

"She also had the duc, her husband, to protect her. You had no one."

"Ah." That was all she said, and Hugh sensed there was a world of meaning in that one drawn-out syllable.

"What does *ah* mean?"

"Nothing."

"It means something."

She stared up at the sky. "It means I understand. You have an obligation to my sister, and you felt sorry for me."

Hugh bristled. He propped himself up on an elbow and looked at her. "I didn't feel sorry for you."

"It's understandable. Everyone feels sorry for me. I'm a young widow. I'm the object of much pity."

"I don't pity you or feel sorry for you. In fact, until a few hours ago, I didn't much like you."

She looked at him sharply, but the scolding words he expected didn't come. Instead, she broke into a smile. "I didn't like you either."

"And now?"

She shrugged. "I'm still considering."

"Bloody hell. What does a man have to do to claim your good graces?"

"It's not as though you like me." She glanced at him shyly. "Do you?"

"I do, actually. I find I like you even more as the night has progressed."

"Really?" Her dark eyes glittered. "Why is that?"

"The mud, I think." His tone was serious but his expression full of humor. "It's hard not to like a woman who slaps mud all over herself without a second thought."

"I had second thoughts. I had third ones as well, but I'd rather be dirty and alive than clean and dead."

"Hear, hear."

"I'm sure most women would feel the same. Not most women of my acquaintance, but most women with any sense of reason."

"The nobility is sorely lacking in reason, I fear."

"But not you. You tried to warn me, to warn all of us, and we didn't listen."

"It's difficult to believe the earth is round when all you see before you is flat."

"I wish I'd listened."

"And what would you have done differently?"

"I might have questioned why so many of my footmen were ill. I might have worried at one of my quartet being absent. Surely these were warning signs for anyone looking."

"I didn't see them, and I was looking."

"It wasn't your household."

True enough, but it troubled him now that there had been signs he hadn't seen.

"Why do you think my servants turned against me?"

"They didn't all turn against you."

"Didn't they? Even if they were not carrying an axe or torch, they didn't warn me. Surely they must have known what was coming."

He didn't speak because he didn't have the answers. He lay back again and looked at the sky, now streaked with traces of pink and orange.

"Thank you," she said quietly.

"There's no need."

"There is. You didn't have to help me. You could have left me in the ballroom."

"And what sort of gentleman would I be then?"

"Perhaps you did act out of chivalry, but I am still grateful."

Hugh should have allowed her to continue with her delusions. He tried to keep his mouth shut, but his body didn't obey the order. "It wasn't chivalry that made me grab you."

"What was it?"

"I don't know, exactly."

That wasn't true. He knew exactly what it was.

"If you didn't like me, then why would you help me, other than chivalry?"

"I might not have liked you, but I'm still a man."

She frowned and then her brow cleared. "Oh," she said simply, her tone full of wonder.

"You find it difficult to believe I might be attracted to you?"

"I suppose I'm not used to thinking of myself in that manner. I've been in mourning for so long."

"And I am a brute for bringing it up."

"No." She sat up, making an adorable picture as leaves clung to her disheveled hair. "I should not say this, but I am too tired to think straight. I like that you are attracted to me. When I first became a widow, I thought my life was all but over."

"Nonsense. You're young and beautiful. You will marry again."

"It's not marriage I miss so much." She turned away from him, but not before he saw the flush on her cheeks. She had been a wife and was therefore no innocent. If she blushed now, it must be because her words were too forward. Which meant he understood them completely. She missed a man in her bed. At any other time this would have been welcome news to Hugh. But here in the woods, potentially surrounded by mobs of angry peasants, there was not much he could do to satisfy his lust or hers.

"As I said, you are young. There will be other men."

"I think it's a sin to want…what I want."

He sat and took her hand. "It's not a sin to be human and have human needs and desires. You've been through an ordeal, and at a time like this, you need comfort."

Her gaze met his, and he realized how his words could be taken. He should squeeze her hand or kiss her knuckles and say that at least he could provide that, but he wanted more. He looked at her face, pink in the dawn, her mussed hair, and the creamy expanse of flesh exposed below her neck, and he could hardly resist. Cupping her chin, he leaned down and brushed his lips over hers.

She was absolutely still as he kissed her, so very lightly, once, then twice. And then her hand was on the back of his neck, cupping it tightly and pulling him closer. Heat surged between them, and when their mouths met, the kiss seared them together. Frantic lips, hot, probing tongues, and nipping teeth made his senses reel. He'd kissed women before, but never like this. Nor had he ever been kissed like this.

Suddenly, the exhaustion, the thirst, the ache in his feet didn't matter at all. He put his arms around her and pulled her close and there was nothing in his world but the scent of apples and pine and the heat of her soft body merging with his. Hugh could think of hundreds of ways he'd like to pleasure her in that moment. He could think of even more that would be mutually pleasurable, but he pushed them all aside and grasped at whatever wits remained. Forcing himself to exercise restraint, he pulled back from her.

The comtesse—he should probably think of her as Angelette after that kiss—stared at him with unfocused eyes so blue as to be almost violet. She gasped in a breath, her chest heaving as though she'd been running for miles.

"I apologize," she said. "I don't know what came over me."

"Whatever it was, it overtook us both. We're both exhausted and tense. We were not ourselves."

She gave him a long look as though to say she had been acting exactly as herself. Did she always kiss like that? Was she always so passionate?

*Not helpful thoughts, Daventry,* he reminded himself.

"It will be light in an hour or so." She glanced at the dove-gray sky. "Do we still try for Versailles?"

Hugh took his time before answering. Now that the sun was rising, he was reminded that he was supposed to have departed for Calais in the morning. Had his man escaped the château? Daventry had no way of knowing. He might still start for Calais, but how could he go back to England and leave her in France unprotected?

Of course, if she refused to go, there was little he could do to force her. As he was not a relative and she was more or less an independent woman, he had no authority over her actions.

"I would rather we start for Calais," he said carefully. "I can secure us both passage on a packet to Dover."

Her brows lowered. "You want me to leave France? Run away as though I am the one who has committed a crime?"

"It's not safe—"

"My friends may be dead. I owe it to them to stay and make certain those who killed them and burned my home are punished."

He shook his head. "You really are blind, aren't you? Don't you see what is happening? This is just the beginning. The lower classes have been oppressed for years. They will rise up and take their revenge by the only means available to them—blood."

"The king—"

Hugh jumped to his feet. "By your own admission, the king is weak and indecisive. It may be too late for him already. It may be too late for all of you. After all, the Third Estate vastly outnumbers both the clergy and the nobility. Look at what happened in America." He pointed in the direction he assumed was west. "Revolution is in the air, and once it takes hold, you and your precious friends will be wiped away."

She rose to her feet. "That may well be. And if the peasants do revolt, I can hardly blame them. I've seen some of the abuses and hardships the poorest of this country have suffered, but not every member of the nobility has treated his or her tenants and servants abominably. Some of us have advocated for reform. Some of us are kind and compassionate."

"And you will die alongside the cruel and unfeeling."

Her shoulders straightened. "Then so be it. I won't leave my friends when they need me the most. If you are for Calais, then go. I will travel to Versailles alone."

She lifted her skirts and marched away. Hugh watched her go, then turned and started toward what he assumed was Calais. If she wanted to die, let her die. But he had responsibilities and duties in England, and he had done what he'd promised her sister. He had tried to persuade her. There was nothing in France to keep him.

# Five

Angelette was so angry that she'd walked for several minutes before she realized she had no idea whether she was turned in the direction of the palace or not. She had to stop and think this through, but it was difficult at the moment when she was boiling with rage inside at Daventry. She should never have kissed the simpering coward. A few shots had been fired and he fled before ever returning fire. She would not run, could not run. She might be half English, but France was her adopted country. She must warn the king and her friends and relatives. She must see them safe.

She looked about her, but nothing in the woods surrounding them looked familiar. A similar perusal of the sky also provided no clues. She might as well be walking in circles. She had to find the road and follow it to the Palace of Versailles. That was the only way. The sun would be up in an hour or so, and she could see which way was east from the direction it rose. The palace was north of her château, and the woods Daventry had led her to were south. It stood to reason if she walked north, she would eventually find herself either at the palace or on the road to the palace. After a quick calculation, she turned herself north and began to walk.

But now that the sky was lightening she did not have to concentrate so completely on where she stepped. She could see the roots and low-hanging limbs to avoid. She had far too much time to think about Daventry.

She'd been right to dislike him. Why had she changed her mind? Why had she kissed him? She must have been, as he'd tactfully suggested, overwrought. But then he was overwrought as well because he'd kissed her back just as passionately. Even now the memory of that kiss made her toes curl and her cheeks heat.

Too much time to think, indeed. She should think about what she would say to the king and queen. She should devise an explanation to give to the palace guards when she arrived in a stained bodice and petticoats. She could only hope they would believe she was indeed the Comtesse d'Avignon. She could only hope she might persuade the king to take action against the men and women who had attacked her friends and burned her house. She must persuade the king that he must act now or risk losing his country.

And of course her thinking was nothing more than wishful. If the king would not listen to his ministers or his brothers, why would he listen to her? Why would anyone listen to her? After all, Daventry had tried to warn her, and she had ignored him and then tried to silence him. Why would the king or her friends and relatives be any different? Perhaps it was folly to stay in France. Perhaps she should have gone with Daventry.

As though her thoughts had conjured him, he stepped out from behind a tree in front of her. She gasped and her heart jumped. "Where did you come from?"

"I circled back around to find you."

Angelette took a calming breath, uncertain whether her heart pounded at the surprise of seeing him or because he was such a handsome man that seeing him could not fail to produce a quickened heartbeat and shallow breaths in her. She could not help but think of their kiss.

*That kiss.*

Angelette closed her eyes and fumbled for control. "If you think to try again and talk me into traveling to Calais with you, you are wasting your time."

"That's not my purpose." He started forward, and she forced her feet to stay rooted in place rather than shuffle back.

"What is your purpose?"

"I wouldn't be much of a gentleman if I left you here in the woods. I'll see you safely to the palace and then make a start for Calais."

"Thank you, but I don't want to keep you from leaving the country as soon as your cowardly legs will take you away."

His hands went to his hips. "It's not cowardice but practicality. I see the storm coming. Even the most foolish would take shelter when he saw the clouds overhead and heard the thunder in the distance."

"So I'm a fool then?"

His hands dropped to his sides. "No. You're loyal to your adopted country. That's as it should be. I have no doubt I would feel much the same were we in England. I'll take you to the king."

He held out his hand, but she didn't take it this time. It seemed more dangerous to touch him than to stumble over a rock. Better to make her own way and not rely on him. After all, she'd learned men were not to be trusted. They left, just when one needed them, and though Daventry had come back, in the end he would leave as well.

An hour later they reached the road. Angelette knew exactly where they were as she recognized the trees as well as a small brook just before the curve up ahead. As soon as she saw it her heart sank. For all the walking they had done the night before, they had not made much progress. The palace was still miles away. They were still very much in danger.

"I suggest we walk in the woods, keeping the road in sight, until we're closer. We can hide among the trees. The road leaves us completely exposed."

She nodded and followed him back into the shaded coolness of the woods. Now that she knew they had miles to go, the exhaustion she'd been trying to ignore crashed down on her. Her aching back and feet would find no relief any time soon. Daventry peered over his shoulder, giving her a questioning look, and she straightened immediately. If he suspected how tired she was, he would want to stop and give her time to rest. She knew they must continue walking. The luck they'd had since the night before wouldn't hold out forever.

They paused at the brook to drink, and Angelette splashed water on her face, savoring the cool wetness on her overheated cheeks. When she rose, she found Daventry studying the brook.

"What's the matter?" she asked.

"It's too deep to cross, and too wide to jump. If we cross it, we'll be walking the rest of the way in wet, cold clothing."

"An unappealing option. What do you suggest?"

He gestured to the road. "We walk on the road until we're past it and then duck back into the woods."

"The problem is that the road curves on that section." She gestured across the brook. "We won't be able to see what's coming or what lies ahead."

He gave her an approving nod. "I hadn't realized that."

"We are left with the option of walking into what might be a trap or trying to make it the rest of the way with wet feet, which will surely blister and rub raw the further we go."

"There's a third choice."

She raised her brows and motioned for him to continue. "We build a bridge across. If I can find a downed branch or limb long enough, we can lay it across the water and walk over that."

Angelette looked about and saw nothing that would suit their purposes. "How long do you think that will take?"

"I think I saw something that might suit our purposes some ways back."

"How far back?" She narrowed her eyes.

"Fifteen, maybe twenty minutes."

"No." She shook her head. "That's twenty minutes back and twenty here again. By the time we have the log in place, we've lost an hour, and then we assume we don't fall off it when crossing and rendering all our efforts for naught."

"A man might wish you weren't half so clever."

"Perhaps a man who wanted to waste time or end up soaked to the skin." Her tone was acidic, but inside warmth spread through her like the morning sunlight. No one had ever called her *clever* before. No one had ever complimented her on anything but her *pretty eyes* or her *lovely complexion* or her *stylish coiffure.* She'd never known she wanted to be complimented on her intelligence...until now.

"True enough," Daventry said with a grin. Apparently, he found her clever and amusing. In a few moments she would forget why she didn't like him again. *Calais,* she reminded herself. *Calais. Coward.*

But he wasn't a coward. A coward wouldn't have come back for her. A coward wouldn't have risked his life to save her in the ballroom.

"So we take the road," she said. "And pray for the best."

He nodded and gestured up the rise that led to the road. "After you."

At the top of the rise, she dropped her skirts and paused to catch her breath. She looked down the road one way and then the other. It was surprisingly quiet and deserted today. The road from Paris to the palace was much busier than the road the local gentry traversed to see the king, but she would have expected to have seen or heard at least one carriage pass now that the sun was up and it was truly morning.

"It doesn't feel right, does it?" Daventry asked from beside her.

"There are no carriages, no horses."

"I have a feeling your château was not the only one the peasants visited last night. I imagine everyone is staying inside."

"Or they're dead."

He looked at her sharply, and she bit her lip. She hadn't meant to say that out loud.

"It's a possibility we may have to consider. I think we'll know more when we reach the palace." His mouth set in a grim line.

"You don't think the peasants could have gotten through the Swiss Guards, do you? They couldn't have hurt the royal family."

"No. I don't think that's likely."

But she heard the note of uncertainty in his voice. She felt it as well.

Taking a deep breath, she stepped out onto the road. It appeared clear in both directions, but of course the curve ahead limited her vision in that direction. She started to walk, but Daventry put a hand on her shoulder. "Let me go first."

She paused to allow him to go ahead of her, half wishing he would offer her his hand again. She would take it this time. She could have used something steady to hold on to. Angelette stayed close to Daventry, keeping his broad back within arm's reach. He didn't walk quickly, but he moved with purpose. She had the urge to run, to glimpse the coming terrain that moment, but she knew it was more prudent to move at a pace that would allow them to backtrack if necessary.

Finally, they rounded the bend in the road, and Angelette sighed with relief. This stretch was as empty as the rest had been. They were still safe. Just a little farther, and they could duck back into the cover of the woods. And then they would reach the palace and be truly safe.

"Not long now," she said, moving more quickly so she might walk beside him. "You will be on your way to Calais and then far away from France."

He glanced at her, but she kept her gaze straight ahead. The sun had risen now, and the day had dawned clear and sunny.

"I hear the censure in your tone," he said. "You think I should stay in France?"

"You obviously finished your business here. Why would you stay?"

"Precisely." He paused in the middle of the road and she paused as well. "This is not my country nor my revolution."

"It's hardly a revolution—"

He waved a hand. "Whatever you want to call it, it's not mine. My business brings me here, but all the wine in the world isn't enough to convince me to risk my life."

"What about the people, then? What about the men and women murdered at my château last night?"

"I feel for them and for their families, but what can I do? I can't save them all. I doubt most even want to be saved as they won't admit they are in any peril. I offered to take you to Calais, but you won't leave. You'll stay and when you finally realize the danger you are in, it will be too late to get out."

"And so I deserve to die? Because I have some loyalty to my adopted country? Because I won't run at the first sign of trouble?"

"Do I deserve to die? This is not my country, and I didn't run at the first sign of trouble. But I sure as hell will run when I have the chance."

"Do that then!" She turned on her heel and marched away.

"I will." She heard his feet crunch on the stones and dirt behind her. Other than that, the day was silent. Too silent. No birds sang. No insects chirped. Perhaps they had been frightened by the arguing. Or perhaps something more sinister lay ahead.

She stopped and Daventry stopped beside her. "I don't like this."

"I was thinking the same thing. We should go back—"

"Stop where you are!" came a shout in French.

Angelette looked about, seeing nothing but green fields on one side and the woods on the other. And then, slowly, men and a few women crept from the trees and out of the trenches on the side of the road bordering the fields. The people were roughly dressed, their clothes stained with soot and what appeared to be blood. In their hands they carried scythes and hedge clippers and even frying pans. They had taken the tools of their trade to use as weapons.

Angelette reached for Daventry's hand, and when he squeezed hers tightly, she knew her assumption was correct. These were the men and women who had burned, if not her home, the residence of someone. Last night she had believed the attackers had come from Paris to invade the wealthy little town of Versailles. But now she could see these were servants and peasants from the town. Their existence was not miserable, not like that of many of the lower classes. But if the discontent had spread to them, then France was in grave, grave danger.

"We have no business with you," Daventry said in French. "We are unarmed and only want to pass this way."

"To go to the palace," a man said. He was one of the first to emerge from the woods. He looked to be a farm laborer, dressed as he was in stained red and white trousers, the rough shoes called sabots, and a red hat on his head. "To report to the king. Your king can't save you now. It's only a matter of time before we deal with him like we dealt with you, *Madame la Comtesse*." He spat the title as though it was a foul brew in his mouth.

So she had been recognized. It wasn't as though she could have hoped that by removing her skirts she would be in disguise. The local villagers knew her. "We only want to pass by in peace," she said. "I've never done you any wrong."

"You ain't never done us any right neither!" one of the women called. She too wore the red cap and the sabots. Her skirt and blouse were covered by an apron streaked with blood. "You never cared about us. While we froze in winter and starved, you ate pastries and warmed yourself by the fire."

Angelette straightened her shoulders. "None of you look to me to be starving. I'm willing to wager that you ate from the table of the master you served and warmed yourself by the fire he provided."

"And put one toe out of line," the leader said, "and a man could be dismissed and destitute. It's time we took some of the power you aristos hoard. It's time we no longer had to bow and scrape just to feed our children."

The men and women around him nodded and murmured. And then the woman raised her frying pan. "Death to the aristos!"

The others repeated the chant and started forward. Angelette squeezed Daventry's hand harder. There would be no escape this time.

Daventry shoved Angelette behind him and held up both hands. "Wait a moment. Let's be reasonable."

"The time for reason is done," the man who seemed to speak for the others cried, still advancing, though more slowly and cautiously now.

"This woman is defenseless and blameless. I can't allow you to harm her."

"We aren't asking for your permission, *rosbif.* Go back to your own country. If you leave now, we'll let you pass unharmed. We want no trouble with the English."

"And what will you do to the comtesse? If you murder her, then you are no better than criminals. You claim you want justice. You claim she has wronged you. She deserves a trial, just as any man or woman would receive."

"We hereby declare her guilty!" the woman cried, brandishing her frying pan. "That's the only trial she needs."

Angelette peered around Daventry's broad shoulders. The leader of the mob looked thoughtful. "You want a trial?" he said to Daventry. "I say we give her a trial. A trial by the people!"

A few men cheered, but most of the mob looked confused. Undoubtedly, they were bloodthirsty and wanted nothing more than to kill her and find the next victim. Even if Daventry managed to give her time by convincing the leader to put her on trial, she was doomed. She still had the knife she'd hidden beneath her petticoats, but what good would it do against this many people? It would have been better for her to run.

"That's exactly right," Daventry said. "Let the people decide her guilt or innocence. Take her into the village and—"

"No!" This time it was the woman who spoke. "We take her to Paris and deliver her to the people there. When she hangs for her crimes, it will be a symbol to the rest of the aristos that the time of reckoning has come."

The leader looked at Angelette and smiled. Angelette shivered. Then his gaze slid to Daventry. "You asked for a trial. We agreed. Give her to me or the English be damned and we take both of you."

Angelette gasped in a breath. Surely Daventry had to realize the trial would be a farce. They would find her guilty and then they would murder her. That was if they didn't kill her before taking her to Paris. Now was the time to run or to fight. She'd rather die fighting than go meekly to her death. Daventry would fight for her.

But to her shock he moved aside, leaving her open and vulnerable. He simply stepped away from her and even before the peasants seized hold of her, she knew she had been wrong about him.

He was a coward after all.

# *Six*

The look in Angelette's eyes as they pulled her away was sharper than a thousand daggers and pierced him just as deeply. But to her credit, she walked without stumbling, keeping her head held high. Dirty hands grasped her, pulling her into the center of the mob, but the peasants were true to their word—for the moment. They led her away without hurting her, walking in the direction of Paris. It was a formality and they all knew it. If she was put on trial, she would be found guilty of any and all fabricated charges.

She didn't look back at him, but Hugh could feel the hatred burning off her. And he could hardly blame her. She thought he had sacrificed her to save himself. Hugh could admit the thought had crossed his mind. He didn't owe her or the nobility of France anything. He had duties and obligations back in England. He couldn't afford to waste time leading French nobles through woods and rescuing them from mobs.

But he hadn't surrendered the comtesse to save himself. He'd done so because there was no other choice. And as long as she was alive, he could still save her.

He watched the mob lead Angelette away. He could easily make out her dark hair in the center of the group. Her back was straight, and she walked gracefully. Hugh wondered if he would have comported himself so well if their positions were reversed. He couldn't help but admire her. He couldn't help but feel more than just admiration. He genuinely respected her.

He turned to walk in the opposite direction, keeping his pace steady but not rushed until he rounded the bend in the road and was out of sight. Then he sprinted into the wooded area and scrambled out of view, lying down to make sure if he'd been followed he would not be spotted. He watched the road for several minutes and when no one appeared, Hugh jumped up and raced through the woods at a dangerous speed, back the way he'd come. He was one man, and it would be easy to catch up to a mob of a dozen or so, but he did not want Angelette out of his sight. He needed to see her, to make certain she was unharmed.

Ignoring the creek that had brought them up to the road in the first place, Hugh ran through it, paying no heed to the way his feet slid in the boots. He ran on, passing matted places in the woods where the peasants had obviously lain in wait. One way or another, he and Angelette would have been caught. Finally, he heard the sound of voices, and he stopped running, cocking his head and holding his breath to listen. He thought it must be the peasants, and he ventured close enough to the edge of the woods to see them. His gaze immediately found Angelette. She walked, chin still in the air, but blood dripped from a cut in her cheek, and Hugh knew she must have been struck.

Anger rose within him, but he tamped it down. He'd hold on to that fury and use it later. Now he slid back into the woods, far enough that he would not be seen but close enough to the edge that he could catch glimpses of the red caps among the peasants. After what seemed a long time, he sighed in relief. The peasants really were taking her to Paris, as promised. He knew the road well enough and, as it was so well traveled, the woods had been cleared to make it safe from bandits who might lie in wait for a passing conveyance. Hugh had no choice but to allow the peasants to walk far enough ahead that he could follow without being detected.

It would take most of the day for them to reach Paris on foot. And then if they were too late, they would have to wait outside for the gates to open in the morning. This would be the best outcome because he could use the cover of darkness to steal Angelette back.

*Walk slowly, comtesse,* he thought, feeling more helpless than ever.

***

Angelette did everything she could to slow the peasants' journey to Paris. She feigned illness, stumbled and fell, and complained incessantly. She was the model of the spoiled comtesse, and by the end of the day she hadn't won any of the peasants' favor. They were especially annoyed at her when they arrived outside Paris to discover the gates were closed for the night. A few of them grumbled about finding a tree and hanging her then and there. No one had a rope, which was probably the only reason she was spared.

The risks she'd taken by angering the peasants today were worth it. Once she was inside Paris she'd be taken to the Palais-Royal and the leaders of this so-called revolution and be killed as an example to other nobles who dared resist. She had to try and escape tonight and enter Paris on her own. Then she could go to the homes of her friends and beg for shelter. She knew it would be offered freely if she could find someone still in the city. Most would be at their country estates in the summer. Perhaps the Vicomte de Merville and his wife would be at home. The vicomtesse was with child and had not felt well enough to travel the many miles to the vicomte's estate.

The peasants built a small fire and sat around it, eating their meager rations. Most had no provisions. Angelette herself had not eaten since the day before and had only managed a few drinks of water from muddy creeks. She was dirty, hot, and hungry, but she didn't complain. She pulled her knees to her chest and made herself small and unobtrusive. The less attention they paid her, the easier to escape. When her captors were done eating, some of them lay down to rest. Angelette lay down too, pretending to sleep. It was difficult not to allow fatigue to overcome her. Instead, she concentrated on listening for the sounds of heavy breathing that would indicate those around her had fallen asleep.

After what must have been hours, all was quiet and Angelette opened one eyelid a sliver. A couple of men stood off to the side, keeping watch and smoking. Their backs were to her, but one turned to glance at her. She closed her eyes again and breathed slowly and rhythmically. When she opened her eyes again, the man was looking away. Now was the time to creep away and into the dark, except that at that moment someone emerged out of the darkness and slinked into the clearing. He stepped over the sleeping men and women and approached the guards without making any sound. What was the man doing? If he was a thief, why not rifle through the pockets of those sleeping? He seemed intent upon those watching over the camp. One false move and he might wake the entire group. Should she run now while she still had a chance or wait and pray the man succeeded in his plan—whatever that might be?

Angelette had had enough waiting. Just as the man reached the first sentry, she rolled over, jumped to her feet, and started away. She'd intended to run, but she'd lain so still for the past few hours that her legs cramped. She fought the sting of needles as her muscles protested and limped into the shadows as quickly as she could. What a fool she'd been. She'd walked all day and her body was not used to so much exercise. She should not have been so still. Of course her muscles had seized up after so many hours of sudden inactivity.

Angelette stumbled into the darkness, finally giving in to the pain and slumping with a hiss behind a broken wagon someone must have abandoned at the gates. Heart pounding furiously, she gritted her teeth and pressed her body against the wheel of the wagon. She could not stay here. The guard was sure to notice her absence in a moment and raise the alarm. She just needed a moment's respite to allow the cramps in her legs to ease. Slowly, she stretched out one leg, stifling a groan. She began to massage the tight calf muscle when she heard footsteps approaching.

Panic welled within her. She would not be captured again. She'd rather die here and now than be paraded through the streets of Paris or murdered by a mob of bloodthirsty peasants. She fumbled under her petticoats and closed her fingers on the knife she'd taken from the stables. Clasping it in her hand, she readied to strike.

The footsteps came closer, and she raised the knife just as the man came around the wheel she used for shelter. She lashed out and would have stabbed him in the thigh if he hadn't caught her arm. A scream rose in her throat, even though she knew she needed to remain quiet, and his other hand closed on her mouth. He yanked her down again, sinking with her and pulling them both behind the cover of the wheel.

Angelette struggled to free herself, but he held her tightly, squeezing her wrist until she finally let go of the knife. Now she was defenseless. She would be raped…or worse.

"Why are you running away from me?" the man hissed in her ear.

She knew that voice.

Daventry.

She tried to say his name, but his hand was still covering her mouth.

"Quietly, yes?"

She nodded.

Slowly he removed his hand from her mouth, but he kept his hand around her waist.

"What are you doing here?" she whispered.

"Rescuing you." His tone was pedantic, as though his purpose should have been patently obvious.

"I don't need rescuing from you. I was rescuing myself. Not that I'd have to rescue myself if you hadn't handed me over to the peasants in the first place. Get your hands off me."

He released her, putting distance between them. She should have been glad, but she actually missed the feel of his body pressed to hers. He felt safe and strong. Without looking at him, she felt in the darkness for her knife and clasped it again.

"What choice did I have but to let them take you? They would have killed us both, and I knew if I followed and waited for the right time, I'd get you back."

She turned to him, trying to see his face despite the darkness. "And how were you planning to stop the mobs in Paris from murdering me?"

"I was hoping you'd manage to stay out of Paris. You didn't disappoint."

She shouldn't have felt pleasure from his words. She was angry at him. She wanted to berate him further for handing her over. Instead, warmth curled inside her. She should have known he would come for her. Why hadn't she trusted him?

"Now is the time to start for Calais. Before the guards I hit over the head wake up."

Ah, this was why she hadn't trusted him. Because he was always trying to run away. "I told you, I cannot leave the country. I have friends and family here. I can't leave them behind. Not until I warn them of the danger."

"Then write them a letter from London."

She scowled at him. "Why did you even bother to come after me? I have told you over and over again, I will not go to England with you."

He rose, careful to stay low and out of sight. "Then I'll go without you."

"Adieu." She turned away from him, looking for a good place to hide when the sun rose.

Daventry sank back beside her. "I'll go after I make certain you're safe—as safe as anyone can be—in Paris."

Angelette couldn't quite hide a smile of relief. She hadn't really wanted him to leave her. "You don't have to do that."

"I know." The tone of his voice made her turn to look at him.

He lifted a hand and touched her cheek. It was still tender from where one of the peasants had struck her earlier. "Does it hurt?" he asked.

"Not very much."

"I could kill the man who did this to you." His gaze was dark and intense, and she felt unexpectedly self-conscious.

She shifted back, moving just out of his reach. She felt more comfortable thinking of him as the man who had abandoned her, not the man who wanted to protect her. "You seem to want to travel to Calais. You don't need my blessing, but I'll give it if it makes you feel better." Now there was emotional as well as physical space between them.

"It won't make me feel better." He moved closer to her again, his eyes dark and intent on her face. "I might as well admit it. Nothing seems to work."

"What do you mean?" Why had she asked? She did not want to know. She wanted that space between them again. She needed distance from the heat in his eyes.

"I mean, I can't seem to let you go." His voice was low and husky, tinged with ruefulness and desire.

Angelette closed her eyes, trying not to allow the tingling his words had caused to overwhelm her. She felt her face heat and floundered for a response. "While I appreciate the sentiment, Lord Daventry,"—she tried to make her tone light and flippant—"this isn't the best time to court me."

"I don't have any intention of courting you, Comtesse."

She swallowed. Her throat dry. "Then what *do* you intend?"

He looked away and she realized after a long moment that he didn't mean to answer. Why that should make her shiver with anticipation, she couldn't say.

"Assuming we can enter the city tomorrow, what's your plan?"

"I believe my friends the Vicomte and Vicomtesse de Merville are at home. They live on the Rue Saint-Honoré."

"And if they are not in the city?"

She bit her lip, and he raked a hand through his hair. "I was afraid of that. Did your husband have a house in Paris?"

"Yes, but I do not think it habitable. When he died his brother began renovations. With all of the unrest, they might not have progressed very far."

"It's still a possibility if we are desperate." He glanced at her. "Unless…"

She lifted her brows.

"Will it upset you to go there?"

"Why?" Then she understood. "Because of Georges? No. Most of my memories of him are at Avignon, but even those have begun to fade."

"How did he die? If I may ask?"

"A fever." She looked away. "It seemed such a small thing. He was well one day and at death's door the next. He was dead within three days."

She felt his hand on her shoulder. "I'm sorry."

"As am I." And she truly was. For a long time she'd been angry at Georges, angry that he'd leave her alone, leave her a widow at such a young age. He had promised to grow old with her. But she felt little trace of that anger now, just a sadness at what might have been. She had mourned him, and while in those first weeks she might have felt life would never go on, now she saw that it did. Now she had a reason to go on.

Perhaps Georges was part of the reason she had so detested Daventry at first. Daventry had reminded her she was still a woman. She'd noticed him, been attracted to him, felt her body come alive again. Daventry was more confirmation that Georges was truly gone and she was still here. Still alive. And she had her whole life ahead of her.

"We'd better find somewhere else to hide. I passed a farmhouse a mile or so ago."

"I'm not certain they'd welcome me or any noble."

He gave her a long look. "I wasn't planning on knocking on the door, Comtesse. We can rest in the stable until sunrise."

"The stable?" She wrinkled her nose.

"The option for Calais and then London is still open."

She sighed. "A stable is fine."

***

Angelette didn't sleep at all. She couldn't have said whether that was because the hay scratched and the smell of manure in the stable gave her a megrim or because Daventry slept right beside her. *He* seemed to have no trouble sleeping. And as dawn grew nearer and gray light filtered into the building, she couldn't stop her gaze from straying to him.

How could he be just as handsome now, with straw in his hair, stubble on his jaw, and dressed in wrinkled clothing, as he had been the first time he'd stepped into her dining room? Angelette was certain she looked a fright. But Daventry's unkempt appearance only made him look more attractive. Strange, as she'd always thought she liked well-groomed men. She'd never seen Georges unshaven. If, on occasion, she mussed his hair by running a hand through it, he quickly set it to rights again. Most men she knew were fastidious about their appearance. Daventry didn't seem the least bothered by the mud on his silk coat or the ugliness of the boots he'd borrowed.

Perhaps that was the difference between French men and English men. She vastly preferred French men. Didn't she?

Part of her wanted to burrow into the spot beside him and press her back to his chest. He would be warm and his body would be a comfort. But if she did press herself against him, would he take that as an invitation to kiss her, touch her? Would she object if he did?

Daventry opened his eyes. They looked large and very blue in the dim light. "Do you always stare at men when they sleep?"

"I wasn't staring." She looked away, annoyed that her face felt hot again. "I was about to wake you. We should go before the farmer comes to tend the animals."

He sat up, stretching his arms wide. She couldn't help but notice how that gesture tightened his shirt over his chest. He was muscled and not given to fat. She could see that much before she dragged her gaze away. While he pulled his coat on, she tied her petticoats up to keep them out of the way, then took the ladder down from the hayloft where they'd slept. He climbed down after her, and when he reached the bottom it was hard to miss the long look he gave her legs. She hastily lowered her skirts again.

"There's a cellar around the back. I thought I might climb down and see if I can find something to eat."

Her stomach groaned in protest.

He winked at her. "My feeling exactly."

She followed him carefully in the dark until they reached the back of the barn. She didn't know how he'd ever spotted a cellar there or how he managed to climb down without breaking his neck. But he emerged with a handful of apples.

She took two eagerly and devoured one without even pausing to take a breath. Belatedly she realized how unladylike her behavior must seem, but he wasn't even paying attention. He was eating his own apple. When he caught her looking at him, he handed her another apple.

"We can buy bread in Paris. I have a few sous in my pocket." Fortunately, she hadn't discarded the pockets when she'd removed her skirts.

He shook his head. "There's little bread in the city. The wheat crop was bad. The people are starving. That's part of the reason behind the uprisings."

"They must have some food for those with coin to pay."

"You can get anything for a price, but now might not be the best time to walk the streets laden with bread. I suggest we find your friends. They'll have sent servants to buy provisions. If they're still in the city."

"Not everyone runs away at the first sign of distress."

"Not everyone has an ounce of sense," he muttered. Stuffing a couple apples into his pocket, he gestured for her to follow him. "Speaking of which, once more into the fire."

## Seven

Paris hadn't improved in the week or so he'd been away. If nothing else it teemed with more tension than before. He and the comtesse had had no trouble entering the city in the morning. The peasants who had held her captive were nowhere to be found. Her friends, the young Vicomte and Vicomtesse de Merville had welcomed her unexpected visit, and she had immediately gone to bathe and change and make herself once again presentable. Hugh was sorry to see her back in full dress again. He'd rather liked the way the thin petticoats clung to her legs and the way the low bodice barely contained her breasts when she bent over.

Now she wore a peach dress that gave no hint as to the long, shapely legs it concealed and the fichu at the neck covered all of the creamy skin he'd admired so often the past few days.

The vicomte's valet had managed to find suitable clothing for Hugh as well, and he'd made an excuse to go out into the city.

"Oh, but you must not go out, Monsieur le Vicomte," Merville told him over coffee and pastries at midday. "It is too dangerous."

"Just Daventry, please."

Merville nodded. Hugh doubted the noble was yet five and twenty or that he had to shave more than twice a week. He had pale blond hair and almost colorless gray eyes. His features were fine and narrow, making him look as though he might break if caught in a stiff breeze. His wife was even more fragile. She reminded Hugh of a china doll. Her hair was more red than blond, but she had the same pale skin as her husband, and she was what Hugh liked to think of as dainty. Looking at the vicomtesse made Hugh appreciate Angelette even more. She was strong and brave. If anyone could survive the tumult in France, it was she.

But the de Mervilles would easily be trampled. They were kind and had opened their home without question. Unlike most of the nobles Hugh had met thus far, the de Mervilles seemed to understand the situation in Paris had become dangerous.

"In fact," the young vicomtesse said, looking at Angelette, "we are preparing to leave the city ourselves. I am feeling better, and we thought to travel to the countryside…" She looked away, her hand going to her abdomen and confirming what Hugh had suspected. She was with child. Her husband came to stand beside her, putting his hand on her shoulder.

"But now you say the countryside is not safe."

"I think you will be safer in the city," Angelette said, sipping her coffee. "Here there are troops to protect you."

"But the royal troops do nothing, Angelette," the vicomte said. "Only yesterday the troops clashed with peasants denouncing the king. And what do you think the commander did after the crowds dispersed? He took the cavalry out of Paris to Sèvres!"

Hugh understood the commander's motivation. He did not want to kill peasants and set off more violence. But if the people were marching in support of those advocating revolution, they had obviously turned against the king.

"Surely the king will order them back," Angelette said.

"It may well be too late," Merville told her. "The people are scrambling to arm themselves. They plundered weapons arsenals, and last night they attacked customs posts and Saint-Lazare."

"Saint-Lazare? I thought that was a convent and hospital," Hugh said.

Merville nodded. "The mob took dozens of wagons of wheat and anything else they wanted."

"The royal troops did nothing to stop them," his wife said quietly.

"And now the electors of Paris have agreed to recruit a citizens' militia from the districts of Paris to restore order."

"So the peasants have formed their own army?" Hugh shook his head. The French king had all but lost and the battle had not yet begun.

"They call it a bourgeois militia. I hear they have more than forty thousand men." The vicomte took a shallow breath. "We must leave before they come for us."

Hugh rose. "You are welcome to travel with me. You'll be safe in England, and I plan to leave for Calais as soon as possible."

"We would be in your debt," Merville said.

"Surely you will travel with us," his wife said to Angelette.

She shook her head. "I can't. I must tell my brother-in-law what has happened and do what I can to help him protect the ancestral estate. I think it is what Georges would have wanted."

"Georges would have wanted you to stay alive," Hugh said, slapping the table angrily. "What good are paintings and carpets if you're dead?"

She glared at him. "I could not care less for the paintings and carpets, but I do care for Georges's family. They are my family too."

"Then write to them."

"I have, but I must go to them as well. When tensions in Paris ease, I will travel to see them." She looked at her hosts. "I will not make you postpone your leaving. I will find another—"

"Absolutely not. You must stay here," the vicomtesse told her. "You are welcome, even in our absence."

"Thank you, Marie."

Hugh put his hat on his head. "Excuse me."

"But Daventry! It is too dangerous!" the vicomte called.

"Let me worry about that," he said and jogged down the steps. Anger burned within him. Angelette was a little fool. If he could have, he would have tossed her in a coach, locked the door, and driven her away. Once the anger burned off, he walked aimlessly for some time, wandering the narrow cobblestone streets. Most of the windows were shuttered and the shops closed. It seemed all of Paris was in hiding, waiting with bated breath for what would come next.

Hugh knew what would come next, and he wanted no part of it. He could waste his breath and rail at Angelette again when he returned, but the problem was that despite his arguments, in her place, he would have done the same. She was loyal to her late husband's family, and he admired that more than he wanted to admit. The question was whether he admired her loyalty enough to stick his neck out and stay to help her.

She hadn't asked for his help, but he didn't think she would refuse it if he offered. But to stay…That would be suicide. The mobs would not care if he was English or French. They wanted blood. He felt it with every step he took. He didn't see them, but he felt hungry eyes watching him from the dark windows above the cobblestone streets. The people were starving for bread and for justice. If it would not be given to them, they would take it through any means necessary.

The Vicomte de Merville had been correct that the streets were dangerous, but Hugh had wanted to form his own sense of the mood of the city. It didn't hurt that this gave him the opportunity to spend a little time away from Angelette. He hadn't been jesting when he'd said he couldn't seem to let her go. Something about her drew him to her. At first, he'd blamed it on duty and honor and all the rest of that rubbish. But now he'd done his duty. She was safe among friends and busy writing to others. He'd done as she'd asked, and he still did not want to leave her.

He wanted to kiss her again. He wanted to draw those heavy skirts up and run his hand along her bare calf.

He wanted to take her to bed. Hell, he wanted to take her back to England with him.

Quite suddenly, Hugh needed a drink. He remembered a wine seller he had seen open on another street. He doubled back and stepped into the shop. It was crowded, which didn't surprise him as almost nothing else was open. Hugh bought a bottle and found an empty table toward the back, barely waiting for a glass before he sat, pulled the cork, and took a drink. It was good wine. He might not appreciate the French penchant for coffee, but he couldn't fault their taste in wine. He'd met with a half dozen of his suppliers and shipped several hundred bottles back to England before all hell had broken loose. His mother would be pleased. That was likely to be the only thing about him that pleased her. For years she'd been pushing him to marry. He'd claimed he wasn't interested in marriage. No woman had ever managed to capture his attention for more than a few hours.

And when a woman finally did, of course it was one who not only didn't want him, but who lived in another country and refused to leave.

He took another drink and closed his eyes. Gradually, he became aware of the conversation behind him. The men spoke in hushed tones, but Hugh could hear them clearly enough.

"We have taken possession of the muskets at the Hôtel des Invalides, but we lack powder and shot," one man said, his voice low.

"I heard the commander of the Invalides sent it to the Bastille," another man at the table said.

Hugh dared not turn his head for fear the men would know he had overheard them. Instead, he sat still and drank his wine, pretending he was concentrating on the bottle before him.

"I heard that as well," a third man said.

"Then we need to get inside the Bastille," the first man said.

"How?"

"We rally the people," the first man said. "There's no greater symbol of tyranny than the Bastille. The king imprisons whomever he wants there, political prisoners with no other offense than looking at His Majesty the wrong way."

Another man snorted. "You know as well as I that there aren't but a handful of men in that prison and those who are there are mostly mad."

"But the people will believe what we tell them, and when we have the Bastille under our control, we have the powder and the shot to take a stand. The monarchy will fall and equality will rule the land."

Murmurs of assent followed, and when the men walked past him on their way out, Hugh did not dare look up. He did not want them to see his face.

***

Angelette hadn't wanted to believe Daventry. Even if the conversation he'd overheard at the shop was true, surely it would not come to fruition. Attack the Bastille? The idea was ludicrous.

But so had been the idea of burning her château.

She hadn't known of the unrest in Paris. Tucked away as she was in the little village of Versailles, all of France seemed quiet and well. Was the king even aware of the violence and destruction? If he was aware, would he dither or would he act? She had the awful feeling he would vacillate and waver and wait too long to act, as always.

Was she a fool for remaining here? Very possibly, but that didn't weaken her resolve. She could not abandon her friends and family in what might very well be their time of greatest need.

At dinner, there were only three. The vicomtesse had retired early to unpack and repack, as she would have to leave behind much more than she had originally planned. Daventry and the vicomte had sent a servant to hire coaches and in the morning the three would be on their way with only the essentials. Angelette wished she could go with them. Her gaze met Daventry's across the table, and she wondered if he would miss her or think of her when he reached the shores of England.

After everyone said their goodnights, Angelette returned to her chamber alone. She had tarried on the steps, hoping Daventry might say a private word to her, but he had walked up with the vicomte. She supposed she would say adieu in public tomorrow morning. Now, she sat in her chamber in a borrowed night rail and dressing gown and combed out her hair. The streets of Paris were unusually quiet. The calm before the storm or the peace they had been waiting for?

Someone rapped on her door and, expecting Marie's maid who had come to attend her the night before, Angelette bid her to enter.

But it was Daventry who entered. Daventry in the dark, sober clothing the valet had found for him. The clothing didn't fit him properly, but he still managed to look handsome. His hair was swept back from his face and his cornflower eyes were dark and serious. Angelette's heart thudded and she suddenly found herself short of breath. This was what she had been hoping for, but now that he was here she didn't know what to say, what to do.

It was improper for him to be here, in her chamber, alone with her. But she didn't ask him to leave. She didn't want him to leave.

She took a calming breath. "I suppose you are here to ask me one last time to go to Calais with you." She ran the brush through her hair again, hoping he didn't notice how her hand trembled slightly.

"I've given up on that," he said, closing the door with a final click that made her dart her eyes at him. "You won't leave, and I respect your decision."

Angelette set the brush down. "You do?"

"I do." He crossed the room, his movements slow and sinuous, like a wolf stalking its prey. He stopped behind her, placing his hands on the back of the chair she occupied before the dressing table. She met his gaze in the mirror.

"I even admire your decision. I appreciate loyalty and courage, even if it is foolhardy."

Her cheeks colored. "I don't think I shall take that as a compliment." But, as always, she felt the dual pull of anger and attraction when in his presence.

"I mean it as one." He lifted her hair and ran his fingers through it. Angelette tried not to shiver.

"I hate leaving you on your own."

"I wouldn't want you to stay."

His hand ceased threading its way through her hair.

"I mean that you must do what you think is right, just as I too must follow my principles."

Daventry didn't speak for a moment. His hand caressed her hair again, causing ripples of sensation to flow from her scalp down to her shoulders, and then to settle in her belly. "Then this is our last night together."

"Yes," she whispered. "For now. If all goes well, we may see each other again sooner than either of us think."

"I have no doubt of that. You're a resourceful woman. If anyone can survive the storm coming, you can."

"Thank you. I *will* take that compliment." She pulled her hair out of his hands and began to plait it. Her hands shook.

"If you did not come to try and persuade me to go with you tomorrow, why did you come?"

He leaned down and took her hands in his, stopping the progress she had made on the braid. Angelette looked up and into his eyes as he began to unbraid her hair. "I think you know. I think you wanted me to come to your chamber almost as much as I wanted to be here."

She shook her head.

"I believe you enjoyed that kiss we shared as much as I did. I don't think either of us wants to end this without at least one more kiss…and perhaps more than a kiss."

"More?" she whispered.

He gave her a sidelong look. "Do you really want to play games, my angel? If you want me to leave, say the word. But if you want me to stay…"

Part of her did wish to play games. They would give her time to think, time to talk herself out of what she wanted to do. But she didn't really want to talk herself out of the promise in his eyes, did she? She might not be foolish enough to believe he loved her, though she did believe he felt something for her. If he didn't, would he have done all he had for her? She certainly hadn't made it easy for him. Or perhaps she was making it difficult for herself because she was frightened of allowing herself to feel all she felt for him.

This was her last chance. After tonight, she would lose him forever.

"Say you want me to stay," he murmured.

"I want you to stay. I want you to take me to bed, Daventry." She started to rise, but he put his hands on her shoulders and gently pushed her back down, keeping her in place.

She watched in the mirror as he bent, brushed her hair off her shoulders, and pressed his lips to the curve of her neck. "You may call me Hugh."

Angelette took a slow breath as his lips traced her skin, ending just below her ear. "Hugh, then." Her voice sounded low and husky. "Take me to bed."

He chuckled, his breath warm on her skin. "I've been wanting to touch you for ages."

"You haven't even known me a sennight."

"And every minute I'm not touching you feels like a year."

She rolled her eyes, but heat flooded her belly at his words.

"Mock me if you will, but time has nothing to do with it. I knew the first time I saw you." His hands on her shoulders massaged gently, kneading away tension she hadn't known she'd held.

"Knew what?" she whispered.

"Knew you were different. Knew that, despite my denials, I would do anything to be with you." His hands moved gently but skillfully. "The more I think about it, the more I believe we are meant to be together."

She shook her head. "I don't believe in fate."

He slid the dressing gown off her shoulders, his hands still massaging. "I believe enough for both of us. Your skin." He bent and kissed her bare shoulder. "How is it so soft?"

"A lady never reveals her secrets."

"Then you have secrets? Good. I like surprises." His fingers took hold of the thin strap of her night rail. "I want to see you." He tugged the strap down her arm, revealing the swell of her breast. "All day I've wanted to rip that fichu you wore off and throw it in the fire."

"And there have been several times I wanted to pull your shirt over your head and see what was underneath."

He gave her a roguish grin. "That can be arranged. Later." He tugged the strap down further. "May I?"

Her nipple was already hard with anticipation. "Please."

He reached for the little bow tied at the valley of her breasts. His hands were large and darker in color than her skin as he loosed the ribbon. The neckline immediately dipped, the strap he'd lowered sliding down farther until the material of her bodice caught on her distended peak.

He followed the fabric down, caressing her skin with the backs of his hands. Her skin puckered in anticipation, but he didn't free her nipple. Instead, he reached for the other strap and slid it off her shoulder until it too dropped precariously low. She looked at him in the mirror, and his eyes were on her face. And then, as she watched, his gaze dropped to take in her bare shoulders, her exposed chest, and the tingling skin of her breasts. He reached over her shoulder, and she watched as he tugged the night rail down farther, exposing her to him. Her nipples were dark and hard, the skin puckered from cold and from need. She could feel moisture gathering between her legs. If he could make her feel like this with only a look, what would happen when he touched her?

Slowly, he bent behind her and lowered his head, his dark hair falling over her shoulder. He kissed her neck, moving around from one side to the other. Her eyes wanted to close, but she forced them open. She wanted to see his hands on her. He slid them down her upper arms, then in to cup her breasts.

She inhaled quickly as the heat of his hands on that aching flesh flooded through her. He raised his head, watching her eyes as his hands took her nipples between his thumbs and began to tease them.

Angelette moaned and arched for him. Her sex throbbed, and she squeezed her thighs together to ease the building need. The more his hands worked her, the more her need grew. She closed her eyes, unable to watch the wanton scene in the mirror. She only wanted to feel. It had been so long since she had felt like this.

Abruptly, he rose and pulled her up, turning her to face him. He pushed the dressing gown and night rail over her hips until she stood naked before him. His eyes dropped to the floor and his gaze traveled over every inch of her until he reached her face again. "You look even better than I imagined. Your legs." He sank to his knees, and her own wobbled to see him kneeling there. "It's criminal to cover them up." He put a hand on her calf, molding the shape of it, then sliding upward to rub her thighs. "So soft."

He bent, and to her shock, he kissed her calf. She'd never been kissed there before, but when he reached around and flicked his tongue over the back of her knee, she swayed with pleasure. Then he tucked his hands between her thighs, opening them slightly and then more so he could kiss her inner thigh. He moved up, his kisses lingering on the delicate skin as her breathing grew more rapid and her legs felt weaker. When his mouth met her curls, she tightened her hands into fists. She knew what he was about. She had heard of this, even experienced it briefly in the marriage bed, but when he licked her, parting her with his tongue, she shook all over.

His gaze held hers and he licked again, his tongue tasting her and dragging against that sensitive skin. Spirals of pleasure coiled there and she shook her head. "You want me to stop?" he asked.

"No. I want you to do it again," she murmured.

Gently, he pushed her legs farther apart, his tongue exploring until he found the place that made her whole body come alive.

"Yes, right there," he said, his breath making her pant even harder. He circled that spot with his tongue, licked and teased, until she was practically mewling like a cat. *This*— she had not known about *this*.

He licked her again, then kissed her mound, moving upward to her belly. Angelette glared at him. "Why did you...stop?"

"You wanted to see me without my shirt."

She blinked, uncomprehending. Then she watched as he removed his coat and allowed it to drop to the floor. Next came his cravat and finally he undid the buttons of his shirt. Her body thrummed, her sex pulsed, her skin was on fire. She wanted him between her legs again, and she wanted him naked when he was kissing her there.

"Take it off," she said when he hesitated before pulling the tails from his breeches.

A knock sounded on the door, and she jumped.

"Madame, shall I help with your toilette?"

"No!" she shouted.

Daventry raised a brow. How did he seem so calm and unaffected? She would have to change that.

"I mean, no thank you." She lowered her voice to a polite level. "I do not require any assistance."

"Yes, madame." The footsteps receded.

"I could use assistance. Help me take this shirt off."

He didn't need any help, but she stepped forward anyway, raising the hem and sliding her bare skin against his as she did so. When they were flush against each other, he lifted his arms and pulled the shirt over his head. Now his breathing had quickened, and when he lowered his hands they closed on her buttocks. The humor had gone out of his eyes, and the intensity she saw there made her own breath quicken.

He lifted her, carrying her to the bed, holding her sex against his so she could feel his erection straining within the confines of his breeches. She reached for the fall, eager to feel him slide into her, but he stopped her hand with his, instead lowering her to the bed and coming down over her. He raised her hands over her head, catching them by the wrists with one hand. His free hand delved between them, cupping her. "So warm."

She felt his finger at her entrance, stroking lightly.

"Do you want me inside you?"

"Yes."

His finger slid into her, and she clenched around it, bucking when he moved deep inside her.

"Not yet," he whispered. "You're ready for me, aren't you?"

"Yes. Yes, please."

But instead of opening his breeches and thrusting inside her, he nudged her thighs open. "You're so wet and pink. Do you want me to taste you again?"

Her gaze locked on his, and her legs relaxed open.

"You like my tongue on you." He released her wrist and knelt before her, opening her to his gaze. "Tell me what you like." He licked and laved.

"Yes, yes." Her nipples were so hard they hurt. She massaged them, and when she looked at him again, his eyes were dark as he watched her.

"Come for me. I have to see you."

He licked her again, then circled her small nub over and over until her body bowed and she shook with the pleasure of it. Finally, he pressed his tongue hard to her, and she shattered into blinding shards of white light. His tongue delved inside her and she clenched hard and long until she gasped for breath.

And still the climax went on. Just when she thought it might end, he slid two fingers inside her, and she convulsed again. "Hugh," she panted. "Yes."

And that was when he opened his breeches and she glimpsed his erection. It was long and hard; her breath caught at the sight. His fingers withdrew, and he rubbed the tip of his member against her entrance.

When he rose to remove his shoes and step out of his breeches, the head was slick with moisture.

"May I?" he asked, covering her body with his, his arms taking the brunt of his weight.

She allowed her legs to fall open, and when he slid into her, it was the sweetest pleasure she had known.

# Eight

He'd barely entered her when he had to pause and clench his jaw. Her body was so warm, so giving.

Her breasts heaved. The nipples were dark red, and when he bent to take one in his mouth it was hard and plump. The muscles of her sex clamped on him, and he half wondered if he was about to embarrass himself. He could come inside her without even thrusting. He hadn't expected her to react so completely to his mouth and hands, and he wasn't even sure he could bring her to climax again. But he certainly wouldn't give her more pleasure if he spilled his seed like a randy untried youth.

Her legs closed, wrapping about his hips and urging him deeper.

"I don't want to hurt you."

"You won't," she promised. She lifted her hips, and she was so wet he slipped farther inside. His head swam from the pleasure. He had to find his control. She rocked up, causing him to groan at the sensation. Tightening his hands on the bedclothes, he thought of trees and windows and everything benign he could until he had himself under control.

"Can you take more?" he asked, looking at her face. Her cheeks were still rosy from the pleasure he'd given her. He wanted to watch again as she climaxed, wanted to see the way her eyes darkened and her lips formed a perfect O.

"There's more?" she asked.

He gave her a half-smile, then bent to take her other nipple in his mouth.

"Yes, more," she all but begged. He buried himself inside her, feeling her close around him, all heat and promise. He moved, thrusting gently, and she gasped, bowing so he could take more of her breast into his mouth. He sucked harder and thrust again, withdrawing almost to the very tip of his rod and then, when she cried out in protest, he filled her again.

Her hands were in his hair now as he moved within her, keeping his thrusts slow and even, but the way she moved made that difficult. He could hear her breathing increase, could feel her skin heating. He looked down at her and she tilted her lips up, and he took them. The kiss was just as it had been before. The world seemed to stop and there was nothing but the two of them. Her tongue dipped into his mouth, and he followed with a thrust of his cock. She all but purred as he withdrew. Then she swirled her tongue into his mouth and he copied her movement.

She met each of his thrusts, her breasts grazing his chest, and that was when his control broke. He yanked her up, pulling her onto his thighs so he could bury himself deep inside her. She looked down at him, her dark hair wild and free about her as she held on to his shoulders for balance. He thrust hard and deep this time, and she opened her mouth with a sound that was pure carnal pleasure. He put his hand on her lower back, and she arched, taking more of him. There was nothing but pleasure for him now. Her breasts rose and fell with his thrusts and she moaned and clenched around him.

Sweat beaded on his brow as he tried to hold back the climax. He could feel the vein in his temple throbbing with the effort, could hear her cries becoming more urgent. And then she clenched around him, and he could hold back no more. The world went black as he came hard and completely. He shouted and she straightened, her eyes glazed and her mouth parted in pleasure.

Her hips moved as she rode him now, taking every last bit of pleasure she was owed. He pushed her onto the bed, pushed into her, gritted his teeth as he came and came. Finally, with a shuddering breath, he lay sated on top of her.

Realizing he must be crushing her, he lifted himself up on his elbows and looked down at her. Her eyes were closed, her head to turned to the side, and dark curls lay against her cheek. Slowly, her eyes opened and smiled. "That was…unforgettable."

He blew out a breath, half laughing. "I don't know what you did to me, but unforgettable is an understatement."

She smiled more widely. "Oh, really?"

"In fact, I'd have to say that my ruination is complete."

"You're ruined?" She arched a brow.

"Utterly. You ruined me for other women."

She rolled her eyes. "Oh, I see. Now you will tell me you're in love with me."

He'd already been half in love with her, but he knew he must tread carefully here. "I could fall in love with you. I think I started falling the moment I met you."

"That was lust," she countered.

"Very well. The moment you walked away from me and into that mob of peasants, head held high."

"That was shame."

"How about the moment I put my tongue—"

She placed a finger on his lips. "There's something between us," she acknowledged.

He moved his hips. "I think that's my—"

She laughed. "You are incorrigible."

"Good thing or we wouldn't be where we are. I'm glad you asked me to stay."

"I don't see how I could have refused you."

"In that case, perhaps you will not refuse me if I ask you to go to England with me."

She shook her head. "Not a chance. I must—"

This time he put a finger on her lips. "I can see I will have to do more to persuade you."

"Will you?" she sounded breathless. "I don't think there's anything you can do to change my mind."

"We'll see about that." And he kissed her again.

\*\*\*

In the morning he woke before her and though he knew he should rise and prepare to depart, it was difficult to pull himself from her arms. She was warm and her scent of apples and honey made him want to bury his nose in her hair and make love to her all over again.

The night they had shared wasn't enough for him. He didn't know if three nights or three hundred would be enough. He would probably have to marry her, but the trick would be convincing her of that—this woman who insisted on throwing herself into the path of danger. Perhaps once this madness in France was over, she would reconsider and he could...

The sound of raised voices drew his attention. Had the coaches arrived already? Surely the servants would have roused them. Hugh rose and went to the window, opening the shutters and looking out. The sun was still low in the sky, the day just dawning. The Rue Saint-Honoré was empty but for the flicker of sunlight on the cobblestones below. Dew sparkled on the flowers planted along the walks and in the boxes on the windows, but soon enough the July sun would burn it away.

"What is it?" came a feminine voice, and Hugh turned. Angelette had risen on one elbow, her long dark hair falling over her bare shoulder in a tumult of tangles and curls.

"I don't know. If the attack had begun, surely we would have heard the cannons of the Bastille."

She nodded. "But the people are congregating, marching."

The sound of raised voices lifted and fell, echoing through the early morning stillness. "The sooner we are out of the city, the better."

She pressed her lips together and looked away. "Perhaps you could stay another day."

He shook his head. Crossing quickly to the bed, Hugh took her hands. "I must leave today, *mon ange*. Soon enough the mobs will forget the Bastille and remember how much they hate the nobility. Then there will be no safety anywhere."

She nodded. "I suppose you are correct."

"I am correct. Dress quickly." He stood and pulled on his breeches. "I will see if all the preparations to depart have been made. You can still change your mind. We could be in Calais tonight. Or if the roads are crowded and we do not make good time, we will stay in another town. I have exporters in almost every town or village. They will take us in, and we'll be safe." After pulling his shirt over his head, he gathered the rest of his clothing, bent to kiss her, and went to the door. "I'll wait for you below."

Hugh had dressed and, since he had very little to pack, made haste to find the butler. On the way downstairs, he encountered the vicomte coming up. "How are the preparations?"

The vicomte shook his head. "Nothing is ready. I asked the servants to bring our trunks to the foyer, but they haven't been moved." The two men continued down the stairs, pausing outside the drawing room, which was empty and dark.

"Then have them do it now."

"That won't be easy. I can't find any of them."

Hugh closed his eyes. It made sense. When he'd heard the sounds of the crowds gathering somewhere in the city, the house had been far too quiet. He should have heard the servants bustling about to prepare for the day. "They've left in the night."

"All but a few maids and my chef. The maids are too scared to speak. My chef just curses and calls the others imbeciles."

French chefs were notoriously arrogant. It didn't surprise Hugh that the chef thought himself better than the other servants. But a few maids and a haughty chef would be of little use. "We'll have to move the trunks ourselves. Do you think the coaches were ordered?"

"I don't know. I sent my man with the money, and he returned with the bill. I have no reason to believe he lied."

"Then we proceed as planned." But now they had an added worry. If the servants had turned against them and the mob decided today was a good day to kill more nobles, then the Merville servants knew the vicomte and his wife planned to leave Paris. They could send the mobs after them. Hugh could only pray the people were too busy at the Bastille to think of the hated nobility that day.

Hugh and the vicomte moved the trunks themselves. By the time they had finished, the day had dawned and the heat was stifling. Shouts and chants had sounded all morning long, but there had been no firing from the guns of the Bastille. "What time were the coaches to have arrived?" Hugh asked.

De Merville checked his pocket watch. "They are already late."

Hugh's chest felt heavy with dread.

"We should eat something before our journey," the vicomte said. "At least we still have our chef."

In the dining room, the vicomtesse and Angelette sat drinking coffee. Both were dressed in traveling clothes and bonnets, which gave Hugh hope. He might have wished they looked less like nobility, but even dressed as servants the women would stand out. They were too clean, too pretty, too elegant. The vicomtesse looked pale and worried. Angelette looked resigned. "No coaches?" she said, not sounding surprised.

"I am certain they are but delayed," the vicomte said with a smile. "Surely they will be here before we are finished eating." He poured himself coffee and filled a plate. Hugh wasn't hungry, and he would never understand the French love affair with coffee. He would have asked the chef for tea, but he didn't intend to drink it.

"What sort of conveyance do you own?" he asked.

The vicomte shook his head. "A small phaeton for use in town and one town hack. That is all."

The phaeton wouldn't even fit all four of them much less any of the de Mervilles' luggage. And that was assuming the servants hadn't taken the horses when they departed. "Then if the coachmen will not come to us, we will have to go to them."

The vicomtesse set her coffee cup down with a rattle. "But surely you cannot think to go out into the city. You could be killed."

Hugh considered. "The Bastille is to the east, just outside the Faubourg Saint-Antoine. I assume your man ordered the coaches in the Palais-Royal, which is west of us."

"Yes. Everything can be obtained from the Palais-Royal."

Owned by the Duc d'Orléans, the Palais-Royal was full of coffee shops, merchants, and at night, prostitutes. The duc took a portion of all sold there and had become a very rich man. But the area had also become a gathering place for those espousing revolutionary ideals to speak and distribute pamphlets. Crowds often gathered there to listen to men argue for equality and revolt. The duc had allowed this to go on because he coveted his cousin's throne and saw in the people a way to overthrow King Louis XVI and take his place.

"Then if the mobs are east and I go west, there should be no danger."

"We go west," Angelette said.

"No." Hugh rose. "It's too dangerous."

"You just said there should be no danger."

Hugh glared at her. "I don't expect any, but if there is, I'd rather you were here."

Now Angelette stood. "And I would rather not stay hidden away. I want to know what is happening as much as you do." She walked past him and out the door of the dining room. Barely pausing, she glanced over her shoulder. "Coming?"

Hugh gritted his teeth before turning to the vicomte. But perhaps seeing Paris as it was now would convince her to leave with him. "Lock your doors and close the shutters. Do not open the door for anyone but the comtesse or myself."

The vicomtesse rose and took his hands in her small, cold ones. "May God go with you, monsieur."

Hugh nodded grimly, then followed the path Angelette had taken to the foyer. As he joined her on the street below, he heard more shots and breaking glass. Law and order had fled and soon chaos would reign. Hugh prayed God too had not abandoned Paris.

# Nine

Angelette adjusted her tall hat, black with a silk ribbon as the only adornment, to shield her face from the sun. The pale orange redingote she wore buttoned at her cinched waist and was open at the chest and down the front to display her white underdress. The wide lapels and capes on the sleeves made it good for wear in all weather, except perhaps the heat of July in Paris. She'd worried her clothing would identify her as a noble, but thus far the nobility was not being attacked on the streets. As soon as he stepped out of the house on the Rue Saint-Honoré, she made certain Hugh was behind her and then reminded herself to breathe again.

She couldn't stop her mind from wandering back to the night before, when he'd stepped into her chamber and not long after stepped out of his clothing. Now that she knew what he looked like under his dark green coat and tight breeches, it was hard not to imagine taking them off him again.

"You may cease scowling at me like that," she said.

"I don't like this. If something happens—"

She held up a hand. "If something happens, then I'll be at your side. If I'm to stay here on my own, I must see what I'm dealing with."

"True enough."

Surprised by the easy victory, she tucked her arm through his and they began to walk toward the Palais-Royal. The houses on this street were mostly owned by the nobility. Angelette did not know if the residents had fled the city or were in hiding. All was quiet and all was shuttered. She glanced over her shoulder at the de Mervilles' house. It too looked quiet and empty.

"You can do as much good in London—perhaps more even—as you can here. Perhaps if you left, you would be running to something, not away," Hugh pointed out as they strolled. His voice was even and his stride casual, but she did not miss the way he looked right and left, his eyes like a hawk's, alert for any trouble.

She wished she could see the matter as he did, but from every angle she looked, departure seemed to be nothing more than a retreat. "My sister is in London, and my mother lives in the north of England, but my life is here."

"Perhaps you could make a life there."

She scoffed. "Living with my mother? Imposing on my sister and her husband?"

"Living with me." He paused and she tilted her head to see his face from under the brim of her hat.

"I know we threw propriety to the wind last night, but I'd rather not sacrifice my reputation and the honor of my family by becoming your mistress."

"I don't want a mistress." His bright eyes looked down at her, and she wasn't certain what she saw in them. Something warm and inviting. Something that made her want to kiss him again. She blinked. No matter if the street was deserted, she could not kiss him.

"What do you want?" she asked, and her voice did not sound like her own.

"A wife."

Her arm dropped and she stepped away from him, her back pressing against the wall of the house behind her. "Are you…" She swallowed.

"Shall I get down on one knee?"

"But you don't even know me."

He gave her a look of pure incomprehension. "I know you. I know you're stubborn and loyal. You're smart and brave and cunning when you need to be. You're passionate and giving and not afraid to take what you want either. You are everything I have ever wanted."

She stared at him. "But what if we don't suit? I'm irritable in the morning and I like my solitude. I dislike riding, but love long walks. You don't know any of those things. You don't know my favorite color or flower or—"

"I'll have a lifetime to learn. All I really need to know is whether or not you'll have me."

"But…" She sputtered. "Do you even love me?"

He wet his lips with his tongue, and her heart seized, afraid he would say no. "I have never been in love," he admitted. "I can't say that I know what it feels like, but if this is not it, I don't know what is." His gaze, clear and steady, bored into her. "Do you love me?"

"I…"

A shout and the scuffle of feet made both of them turn back toward the direction they had been heading. A group of about six men, boys really, had stepped out from a side street and were marching up the Rue Saint-Honoré. They wore coats, some military in style, and trousers, but most were barefoot. All had small round pieces of red, blue, and white cloth pinned to their breasts.

"Who are you?" one of them demanded as the group neared. "Are you friends of liberty or the enemy?"

Angelette opened her mouth to tell this man that he had no right to speak to her in such a way, but Hugh took her wrist and squeezed. "We are friends of liberty," he said, making his English accent apparent.

"You're British," said the youth, who couldn't have been one and twenty.

"Yes."

The leader looked them up and down. "The British are no friends of liberty."

The men muttered their agreement, moving forward menacingly. Most held some sort of weapon. A few had old muskets Hugh doubted had powder or shot, but many carried kitchen knives or crudely made weapons.

"But we are friends of liberty. That is why we stripped our king of his power years ago and created a constitution and a parliament."

"A parliament ruled by aristos," the leader said and spat. "The people will rule France."

"Then long live the people," Hugh said. He turned to Angelette, his eyes filled with warning.

She could hardly find her voice. "Long live the people," she repeated finally.

"Aristos," said someone in the group of what Angelette now realized must be part of the citizens' militia. "Death to the aristos."

A few mutters of agreement sounded, and Hugh pulled Angelette behind him. Her legs would barely move. This was not the Paris she knew. The boys moved forward, and Hugh stepped back. Angelette closed her eyes, and then the air exploded in a burst of sound that seemed to rock the entire city.

Angelette was thrown against the building. Her hat toppled from her head, and for a moment all she saw was the gray of the wall and the blue of the sky turning over and over. When she regained her balance, she looked up and into Hugh's concerned eyes. "Did I hurt you?"

"I don't think so." She took a mental inventory of all her aches and pains. None were serious. "Did you throw me to the ground?"

He gave a her a rueful smile. "I was trying to protect you. Obviously, I made a muck of it."

She raised her hand to cup his cheek, but the moment was short-lived. The half dozen members of the citizens' militia shouted and jostled and pulled her and Hugh to their feet. "The Bastille! Down with tyranny! Down with the Bastille!"

Angelette was yanked roughly to one side and Hugh to the other. Another boom resounded over the city, and Angelette realized it must be the cannons of the Bastille. Was the garrison there really under siege?

"Let us go," Hugh was saying over the ringing in her ears. All around them, people had come out of their houses. Doors had opened, windows were raised, and Paris lifted its head to peer about.

"We haven't done you any wrong. We only want to go to the Palais-Royal."

"You're coming with us," the leader told them, motioning his men. Angelette was grabbed roughly and pulled forward. "Our troop leader is at the Bastille. He can decide what to do with you traitor aristos!"

Angelette tried to protest that she wasn't a traitor, but the men didn't listen. She was dragged along with them, past the de Merville house, along the Rue Saint-Honoré, and closer and closer to the roar of the crowds at the Bastille.

*\*\*\**

Hugh knew as soon as they arrived that the situation was serious. From the little conversation he overheard, he surmised that a group of peasants had been shown inside the fortress to negotiate, but as the negotiations dragged on, the crowds had grown impatient and attacked the fortress, gaining entrance into the undefended outer courtyard.

He and Angelette were thrust into the midst of the crowd, surrounded by men and women with pikes, who shouted and screamed and pushed to enter the Bastille. People pushed against them on all sides, screaming and jostling, and it was all Hugh could do to hold on to Angelette and keep his footing. Then the soldiers fired on the crowds. Everyone screamed and ducked down. Some ran for cover, but others rose from overturned wagons and behind walls and fired back. The cannons fired again, shaking the entire city and making Hugh's ears ring. Choking smoke rose from windows of the Bastille and drifted into the courtyard where the mob had managed to set fires and obscure their activities.

Hugh coughed into his sleeve and fought to keep Angelette close. If he could only find an opening, he could take her and disappear into the crowd, but not only were the crowds too thick, the small militia holding them captive were attentive. He should have fought them earlier—six against one were steep odds—but now he had no chance. He and Angelette were dragged along, closer to the courtyard and the fighting as the boys of the citizens' militia searched for a leader to whom they could present their spoils. Hugh was taller than many of the other men and he could make out the fallen drawbridge that had been the barrier between the Bastille's courtyard and the outside. As they neared it, pushed inexorably along, he dragged Angelette against him, using his body to shield her.

"This is madness!" she cried as the crowd surged, and she was crushed to him. "They will never take this fortress."

But Hugh was not so certain. The royal army had stood by when the people had attacked the Hôtel des Invalides. What was to compel them to act now? Moreover, as Hugh understood it, the Bastille was manned by former soldiers who were too old or infirm to carry out the duties in the regular army. How long could they stand if faced with a lengthy siege? Yes, there were Swiss grenadiers inside, but what good were thirty or so against a thousand?

More musket fire erupted from the Bastille, and the *vainqueurs de la Bastille,* as the people were calling themselves, retreated, pushing Hugh and Angelette back as well. For a moment, they were separated from the militia, and Hugh looked for a place to take cover and stay hidden. But just as he slid along the wall of the Bastille, a hand grabbed his shoulder and two of the boys from the militia shoved him forward.

"This way, aristo!"

"They'll kill us," Angelette said as once again they were pushed by the flood of *vainqueurs* over the fallen drawbridge and into the courtyard.

"They're too busy taking the fortress to worry about the nobility today," he answered. Still, he would rather not test that premise.

Finally, Hugh and Angelette stumbled into the courtyard, where they were jostled toward a makeshift barricade of carts and barrels. Hugh pulled Angelette down, keeping his head low while a barrage of pistol balls flew overhead.

"Watch them!" the boy heading the citizens' militia told two of his men, and he moved into the smoke and chaos to seek out his leader.

The two boys stood guard over Angelette and Hugh, occasionally ducking down when another volley of fire opened. It seemed an eternity that Hugh sat in the shadow of a cart while the battle raged around him. The hot sun beat down, the heat made worse by the stifling smoke from the fires and the cannons. The mobs threw rocks and fired their weapons, making attempts to storm the gates to the inner courtyard. The attackers had several cannons, but as Hugh watched, two more cannons were rolled into the courtyard, manned by men who were clearly French army troops who had changed sides.

The cannons were heavy, and the men struggled to move them forward, but it was obvious that they would eventually succeed. "That's the fall of the Bastille right there," Hugh told Angelette. She looked up from where her forehead rested on his chest, then burrowed into him again.

"These are the aristos, sir."

Hugh looked up to see the youth had returned with a man in uniform. Despite obviously having been among the *vainqueurs,* his coat was still clean and stiff, his trousers unsoiled, and his hat neatly on his head. He wore the same red, blue, and white fabric pinned to his coat, but he appeared further up the ranks as he wore boots and had not only a sword but a pistol tucked in his belt.

The citizens' militia leader had clear blue eyes, a straight nose, and thin lips. Hugh thought his hair might be light brown or blond, but it was difficult to tell. He was of medium height and build, nothing out of the ordinary, but when he looked at Hugh, Hugh straightened.

"You've done well, citizen," the leader told the boy. "These aristos might have foiled our plans today."

Angelette looked up. "Foiled your plans? We wanted nothing more than to hire a coach to take us away from this place. We wanted nothing to do with the Bastille or—"

"Silence, woman!" the leader bellowed. "I know a lie when I hear one. Stand up." He motioned to Hugh, and Hugh stood, pulling Angelette up with him. "I'll take these two with me to the Hôtel de Ville to stand trial." He withdrew his pistol and gestured to Hugh to move forward. "You stay and fight. Today your names will be recorded along with the others as the heroes of Paris, *vainqueurs de la Bastille* and of tyranny!"

"Death to tyranny!" the boys from the militia called, and their cries were answered by others around them.

The leader pushed Hugh forward, and the three fought their way back through the crowds still swarming into the courtyard. Hugh leaned down to speak close to Angelette's ear. "As soon as we are away from these crowds, we run."

"He has a pistol," she muttered back.

"By the time he primes it, we can be out of range. Trust me. We run." Besides, he preferred a shot in the back to a sham trial at the Hôtel de Ville. They pushed their way through the people swarming to the Bastille, finally pausing at the far wall of the fortress. The crowds were thinner there, and the wall blocked the view of anyone passing by.

"Halt," the captor ordered.

"Bloody hell. Now what?" Hugh muttered. They were so close to being in the open where they could run. He stopped, keeping Angelette tucked into his side.

"Turn around," the solider said.

Quite suddenly Hugh was not at all certain this man had ever intended for them to reach the Hôtel de Ville. What was to stop him from shooting them here on the street? Hugh turned, pushing Angelette behind him. The man standing behind him held no pistol. He'd tucked it away and removed his hat.

With a lopsided smile, he gave them an exaggerated bow. "Well, sink me. I thought we'd never escape all that smoke and noise."

# *Ten*

Angelette stared at the man smiling before them. He was handsome, his features aristocratic and his clothing far too fine to have been issued by the military. And he spoke in English.

"Well, don't just stand there and gape at me all fish-faced," he drawled. "Let's go find someplace civilized."

"You're English?" Hugh said.

The man smiled. "And so are you, I see. Good. That makes everything much easier. I won't have to bribe some French officials to give you papers."

"Papers?" Angelette said.

"Yes, to leave France, my lady. I'm afraid it's rather inhospitable to our kind at the moment. Shall we walk?" He gestured to the south.

"We are staying with friends this way," Hugh said.

"Then by all means, lead the way."

They walked for a few minutes and when they were back on a quiet and all-but-deserted street, the man stopped again. "Forgive me, I haven't even introduced myself. Sir Percy Blakeney." He bowed again.

"Hugh, Viscount Daventry, and this is the Comtesse d'Avignon."

Blakeney took Angelette's hand and kissed it. "I'm charmed. Shall we?" He indicated the boulevard, and they walked on. "If you don't mind my asking, how is it you ran afoul of those wayward youths?"

"My friends, the Vicomte and Vicomtesse de Merville, wanted to leave Paris this morning, but the coaches they ordered never came," Angelette said. "Lord Daventry and I set out for the Palais-Royal to see if we could discover what had become of the vehicles, but we were intercepted."

"I see. We shall have you back on your way soon enough."

Angelette glanced at Hugh. This was all too strange and too impossible. "But we are in your debt, sir. How is it you came to be at the Bastille?"

"I heard all the shouting and firing this morning and thought I would pop in to see what the commotion was about."

"Pop in?" Hugh drawled. "Dressed as a soldier?"

"One does like to blend in."

"Of course," Hugh said wryly. "And does one also like to rescue aristos in jeopardy?"

"I haven't made a habit of it," Sir Percy admitted, "but I suppose it's as good a hobby as any other. There's an actress here I'm rather fond of, but one does need something to occupy one's time when she is not on stage."

"Are you not worried you will be arrested?"

"Lud, no. These Frenchies have enough trouble without angering the British government."

"The boys who took me into custody today didn't seem concerned about the British government."

Sir Percy shrugged. "I suppose you are correct, but I'll have to take my chances. The actress, you know." He sighed rather dramatically.

They walked on, listening to Sir Percy go on about his actress, a Marguerite St. Just, and bemoan the lack of tea and decent tobacco in Paris. Hugh agreed on the tea, while Angelette kept her own counsel. She was still trembling, her ears ringing from the boom of the cannons. She might have died today. A stray pistol ball, an angry *vainqueur,* a real militia leader who had decided it was more expedient to shoot her rather than take her into custody.

She should have been more eager than ever before to leave Paris, but she couldn't help looking at the shuttered windows of the Rue Saint-Honoré and wondering who would be next. And who would save those men, women, and children?

They reached number thirty-three, and though Sir Percy would have left them, she begged him to stay and at least take some refreshment. Hugh assured him the de Mervilles had tea, and the matter was decided.

After a reunion with the distraught de Mervilles, who thought the worst—and rightfully so—when Hugh and Angelette had not returned, the small party sat down to take refreshment, while outside the boom of the cannons started again.

"That will be the two cannons the *vainqueurs* brought in," Hugh said. "It won't be long now."

"What will the king do?" the vicomtesse asked.

"I imagine he'll go hunting." Sir Percy had removed his gloves to sip his tea, and she noted his gold ring had been carved with a small flower. It reminded her of a necklace she had, but which had now been lost to the fire in her château. Her mother had given it to her, and it was made of small gold plates with carved roses on them, supposed to depict the white and red roses that symbolized the houses of Plantagenet and Lancaster.

"Is that a rose on your ring, Sir Percy?" she asked.

He glanced down at it. "Lud, no. It is a pimpernel, nothing more than a humble wayside flower."

"And why do you wear it?"

"It grows in abundance near my estate, and I'm rather partial to it. Bright red when it blooms, you see, and I've always been partial to scarlet."

The man was altogether rather silly. Or, perhaps, like the military uniform, that was an act. But he had managed to save her. And he had said he might as well do something between visits to the theater. Perhaps he could make certain the de Mervilles left Paris safely. Perhaps he might help her brother-in-law escape as well.

Angelette suddenly lowered her cup of coffee. The saucer rattled so that everyone in the room turned to look at her. Her hand trembled, but she dared not lift the cup and saucer to set it on the table. She feared she would dump the contents on her skirts. She swallowed. "Sir Percy, when you first met us, you mentioned the trouble with acquiring documents. Have you done that before? My friends"—she gestured to the de Mervilles—"will need passports in Calais."

He shrugged. "Easily done, madame. I have a friend who is quite good with reproductions."

*A polite way of saying he knew a forger,* she thought.

"And you say you have helped others escape the country?"

"A few here and there. Innocent men and women who found themselves in prison for no apparent reason."

"You broke into a prison?" Hugh sputtered.

"Sink me! I would hardly characterize it that way. I merely walked in one way and walked out another. It's not as if the jailors were paying attention, and for the price of a few sous, they can be easily distracted."

Angelette nodded, but Hugh was already shaking his head. "I can see what you're thinking, and it's a bad idea."

"Why?" she demanded. "Someone has to help, why not me? Why not us?" She gestured, encompassing all of them. "The situation here will only grow worse. I have funds as well as jewels safe with my solicitor and Sir Percy obviously has a knack for extricating people from difficult situations."

"Even after all you saw today, you won't think of leaving for London?" Hugh asked.

Angelette swallowed. "I can't run away when people need me. Once the Bastille falls, the so-called bourgeois militia will seek other targets of tyranny."

"Exactly why you should be far away in London."

"But that's just what will keep me shielded. I'm half English. I can claim English citizenship. The peasants want to punish *French* nobility."

Hugh stood. "Are you forgetting you were married to a French nobleman and carry that title?"

"No, but I don't have to use it. Sir Percy could acquire papers for me."

"I could—"

"Stay out of this." Hugh pointed to Blakeney before rising and crossing to her. "Angelette, you must see now that it's too dangerous to stay."

"I have to agree," Sir Percy said, rising. "If the king does not act after the fall of the Bastille, even I may be forced to return to England for a few weeks. In the meantime, allow me to arrange coaches for you. I will return in the morning to see you off."

Angelette rose as well. "Thank you, Sir Percy."

He took her hand and bent to kiss it, but his gaze remained fixed on hers. "I am at your service, madame."

Angelette nodded. She understood him perfectly.

***

Angelette sat with Hugh and her friends in the de Mervilles' shuttered drawing room listening to the sounds of cannon fire. The Vicomtesse de Merville finally had to lie down. She shook so with nerves each time the cannons fired.

But Angelette found the silence that descended sometime between half past five and six even worse than the sound of the cannons. Was the siege over? Who had won? An hour passed or maybe more. The chef came to ask when they would like to eat, but no one had any appetite. Finally, Daventry could sit no longer. He went to the shuttered window overlooking the street and pulled it open. The vicomte soon joined him, both men staring out at the deserted street, looking for answers that were not there.

"I will walk down toward the Bastille and see what we discover," Hugh said.

"Monsieur, I beg you not to." The vicomte wrung his hands. "It is too dangerous."

"I'll be careful." He started for the door, then gave Angelette a hard look. "Stay here and don't open the door for anyone but me." He walked out of the drawing room and she followed. At the landing for the stairs, she grasped his coat.

"Be careful."

He smiled down at her. "So you are worried about me."

"I'm terrified for all of us."

He cupped her chin with his hand. "No one would ever know it by looking at you. You look as cool as one of Gunter's ices."

She swallowed. "I'm not made of ice, though. And I don't want to lose you."

"I'll be back." He bent and kissed her softly. "That's a promise. Lock the door behind me." Then he released her and was gone.

She locked the door and returned to the drawing room where the vicomte pressed a glass of wine into her hand. "Drink this. I think we both need one."

She drank and paced and drank and paced. She went all too frequently to the window to look out, but the few people on the street were not familiar to her. She was walking away from the window and checking the time on the bracket clock once again when the door burst open and a servant entered.

"Forgive me, Monsieur le Vicomte."

"What is it, Pierre? You have heard news?" Her host set his wine on a table. Angelette sank into the closest chair. Her knees were weak with worry for Hugh and fear for the city and the people of Paris.

"Yes, Monsieur le Vicomte. The Bastille. It has fallen."

"Mon Dieu."

"Are there any casualties?" Angelette asked.

The servant turned and bowed to her. "I do not know, Madame la Comtesse. I think there must be some." He looked back at his master. "Shall I go find out, Monsieur le Vicomte?"

"No. Stay here. Stay inside and be safe. We will all stay inside tonight."

"Yes, Monsieur le Vicomte." He bowed and was gone.

"I cannot believe the Bastille has fallen," de Merville said, sitting and running a hand through his fine hair. "How can this have happened?"

Angelette went to sit beside him. "You did not see the people. There were a thousand or more, and when we escaped they were bringing in cannons. I do not see how the *invalides* could have held out without the support of the army."

"The army." De Merville shook his head. "They are worth nothing." Suddenly, his head shot up, and he looked at Angelette, then at the window.

"What is it?" she asked, but then she heard too. It was a distant roar that grew louder by the second. The sound of a great crowd coming nearer.

Without a word, the two rose and went to the window. They peered out and at first saw nothing but the deserted street. Then a few men carrying flags and crude weapons ran by, quickly followed by more. The crowd was not angry, though. They were singing, rejoicing. Many of them danced in the streets, their limbs covered with soot from fires or gunpowder, some with blood on their clothing.

"Look away," the vicomte ordered. "Angelette, turn away!"

She'd never heard him speak so, and she quickly turned her back to the window. "What is it?" she asked.

"It is too horrible. The peasants have killed the governor of the Bastille and are—no, it is too awful."

Angelette reached for a chair. When her hand did not land on one, she sank to the floor. De Merville pulled the shutters closed, blocking out the noise of the victors and the last of the fading summer sunlight. Night would be on them soon and with it all the horrors of the dark.

He crouched down beside her. "The English viscount will return soon. You need not worry."

"I just want him to return with his head still attached to his shoulders."

He put a reassuring hand on her shoulder. "I should go to Marie. All the noise will have frightened her."

Angelette gave him a weak smile. "Yes, go to her. I will have another glass of wine and wait here for Daventry to return."

"Shall I have the chef send you a meal?"

Angelette knew she would not eat it, but she agreed. The vicomte de Merville did not need to worry about her on top of his other concerns. When he was gone, she poured another glass of wine and then another. When she went back to the window, her head spun slightly from the drink, but it was better than reeling from fear.

The street was darker now. No one had lit the streetlamps and the shadows were long and growing. A few people had emerged from their homes, but they scurried quickly in and out of the patches of light. None walked quickly and confidently, head held high, like Hugh. She gripped the windowsill until her hands were white. She knew this feeling, the wave of helplessness crashing over her. She'd felt it just a couple years before when Georges had become ill. She'd been able to do nothing to save him, and she could do nothing to save Hugh. She must wait and pray and hope for the best.

But all the praying and waiting and hoping had not saved Georges, and she did not think it would save Hugh either. Passivity had not gained her anything. Perhaps it was time to take a more active part in her life and the future of this, her adopted country. If Hugh had not yet returned, then she would go out and look for him. Angelette crossed to the fireplace and took the poker in her hand, brandishing it with a flourish. She'd watched men fencing for many hours and knew some of the methods and techniques. She'd seen women in the crowds of Parisian citizens. If they could fight, so could she.

Poker in hand, Angelette left the drawing room and started down the steps. Her fear did not dissipate, but it felt less all-encompassing. She felt far more powerful and more in control of her destiny. In the foyer, she paused to take a deep breath. She could still change her mind, still return to the drawing room or go to her bedchamber. Instead, she straightened her shoulders and went to the door.

Then she jumped when someone pounded on it. Angelette managed not to scream, but it was a near thing. What if she had opened the door a moment before? Would she have come face-to-face with a mob demanding her head?

"Open the door," a man said softly. "It's Daventry."

Angelette dropped her poker, unlocked the door, and threw it open. She propelled herself into Hugh's arms, almost sending him toppling over backward. She didn't notice. She didn't care about anything except that he was alive and safe and *here*. "Where have you been? Are you hurt? What took so long?" she demanded. And then before he could answer, she kissed him with all the passion and relief she felt in that moment.

She was vaguely aware that he carried her inside and closed and locked the door behind them. He kissed her back, finally separating from her when she was forced to breathe.

"I hope I can expect this sort of welcome every time we're apart."

She scowled. "Do not jest, Hugh. I thought you had been taken."

He gestured to the poker on the floor. "And you were coming to rescue me with that?"

"I was frightened. The Bastille has fallen and a crowd marched by with the dead governor."

His expression grew more serious. "I know. I saw them, and I learned they murdered some of the soldiers at the Bastille, though the *vainqueurs* suffered heavier casualties. Nonetheless, they have gone to the Palais-Royal to celebrate their victory."

"Perhaps they will stay there and leave us in peace."

"We are safe tonight." He pulled her back into his arms. "Apparently, you've been celebrating on your own." He kissed her. "You taste of wine."

"I needed courage and something to calm my nerves."

"I admire your courage. I should have used more caution and stayed here. The streets are dangerous."

"You're safe now." She buried her face in his chest, inhaling deeply of his scent. "Will you stay with me?"

He kissed her. "As long as you want me."

"I want you tonight."

Hugh lifted her and carried her up the stairs. "I'm yours."

# *Eleven*

He brought her to his bedchamber, kicking the door closed behind him, then laying her gently on the bed. She smiled up at him as he removed his hat and gloves, then came down on top of her, covering her warm, supple body with his.

Her arms went around his neck, pulling him closer, and her lips parted, enticing him to enter. Their tongues met— exploring, tasting, teasing. She kissed him more deeply and passionately, taking his breath away and forcing him to exercise willpower so as not to push up her skirts and thrust into her like an untried youth. "Slow down," he murmured, pushing her hair off her shoulder and kissing her neck. "We have all the time in the world."

"I wish that were true." She took his face in her hands. "But tomorrow may be our last sunrise. Certainly the governor of the Bastille had no idea today would be his last."

He turned his face and kissed her palm. "I'll protect you."

"And I will protect you. But tonight is for pleasure." She loosened his neckcloth and tossed it aside, then pushed him up until they faced each other on their knees. He hadn't lit any candles and most of the servants had fled, so no fire burned in the hearth. Only the light from the moon illuminated the pale skin of her face and shoulders.

She first removed his coat, then his waistcoat, then teased him by slowly tugging his shirt over his head. Her hands caressed his bare chest, exploring him as though attempting to learn the contours of his shoulders, arms, and abdomen. Her mouth followed where her hands trailed, leaving a hot, wet path over his skin. He shivered and grasped her shoulders, taking her mouth with his and kissing her hard, showing her with his tongue what he wanted to do with his body.

Her hand moved between them, finding his hard length and molding around him. He groaned as she stroked him, then freed him from his breeches. He broke the kiss as her warm hand slid up and down his erection, and he had to gulp in breaths and clench his teeth to keep from coming in her hand.

And then she bent and her wet mouth closed on his tip. Hugh jerked, seeing stars. *"Mon ange,"* he managed, his voice strangled as she took more of him inside her mouth.

Hugh could not take any more. He pulled her up and shoved the shoulders of her dress down. "How do you take this off? You're wearing too many clothes."

She frowned at him. "I wasn't finished."

He lifted then turned her around and began to unfasten the buttons up her back. "Your efforts, while appreciated—*very* appreciated—will end this all too soon and without any pleasure for you."

She glanced over her shoulder at him. "I'm sure you could find a way to make it up to me."

"Another time I'll show you exactly how creative I can be. Stand up." He rose and removed the remainder of his clothing, then slid hers off as well. She bent to remove her shoes and stockings, giving him a lovely view of her bare bottom. He cupped it with one hand, then took hold of her hip and pressed himself against her. "I want you on your knees."

"You shall have your wish," she said, turning. "But not like that. Tonight I take you." She moved, forcing him to turn as well. When his back was to the bed, she gave him a small shove. Hugh could have easily have had his own way, but he allowed himself to fall back, allowed himself to enjoy the sight of her, lovely and naked as she stood looking down at him.

She climbed on the bed, straddling him and resting her hands on either side of his head. Then she bent to kiss him, her breasts rubbing against his chest. Her mouth slanted over his, claiming him as his hands roamed over the curves of her body. His hand moved between them, cupping her sex. She was warm and wet, ready for him. His fingers tangled in her damp curls, sliding inside her, his thumb teasing the nub at the apex of her entrance.

She gasped and lifted her head, her gaze meeting his. "I am supposed to take you."

"You will have your chance." He thrust in and out of her, her hips moving in time to his rhythm. When she arched up, he took one breast in his mouth, sucking her nipple until it hardened to a point against his tongue.

"Enough." She grasped his hands and pinned them to the bed with her own. Hugh gave in, only too glad he had surrendered when she lowered herself onto him, drawing his cock slowly inside her tight sheath.

It was the most exquisite form of torture, and he all but shook with the effort it took not to thrust hard and fast into her. She moved so much more slowly than he would have liked, rocking her hips and taking him inch by inch by inch. When he was finally buried to the hilt she clenched around him, then rose and repeated it all again.

"You're killing me," Hugh said, his voice like gravel.

"You like it," she countered. He couldn't argue. Watching her take him, make love to him, was the most intoxicating experience he'd ever had. And when her face flushed with her own pleasure, and her hips moved faster, he locked his gaze on hers. She rode him hard and fast at the end, her eyes dark and her lips open as she clenched around him. He would have fallen in love with her in that moment if he hadn't already been in love with her.

She collapsed on his chest, breathing hard, and he held her for a long moment, then slid out from under her. On her belly now, she turned her head and gave him a sultry look, lifting her hips in invitation. He grasped those hips and yanked them higher, sliding into her with a cry of intense pleasure. She was so tight and he was so deep within her that his senses reeled. He moved inside her, careful not to hurt her, so wrapped up in the sensation that it took him a moment before he realized she moved with him. She moaned, her hands clenched in the bedclothes, her body thrusting back to connect with his. Hugh tried to slow his climax, but he was too close. Instead, he reached between them and found her small nub, massaging it until she stiffened and thrust back hard.

He came as she squeezed him tightly, her own cry echoing his. And when, after several moments, it was over, he turned her, took her in his arms, and held her close. "You have utterly slain me."

"I think the whole house knows that," she murmured.

He kissed her forehead. "That was not me crying out earlier."

She closed her eyes. "I shall never be able to face the de Mervilles again."

"That will make the morning somewhat awkward."

She pushed at him. "Do not remind me."

"Will they resent me?" he asked. "Were they close friends of your late husband?"

She stilled, then lifted a hand and tenderly pushed the hair out of his eyes. "They were always more my friends than his, but regardless, they will want me to be happy."

"And are you happy?" he asked.

"Immeasurably." He pulled the sheets over them and held her, breathing in her scent as sleep tugged at him. He sensed there was something she was not telling him. He had thought it to do with her late husband, but whatever it was, it was not about the late comte. Perhaps she had decided to leave with him for England. Perhaps they had a future together there. He fell asleep dreaming of that future.

He was awakened what felt like a few minutes later, but must have been hours. A servant pounded on the door. "Monsieur, there is a man here to see you."

"One moment." He disentangled himself from Angelette.

"Who is it?" she called as Hugh pulled on his breeches.

"He says his name is Blakeney, madame."

She jumped up. "Sir Percy?"

"Stay here," Hugh ordered as she dropped her chemise over her head.

"You stay here." She gathered up the sheet and used it like a robe. Hugh was forced to don his shirt as he walked out of the room or be left in her wake.

"Where is he?" Angelette demanded.

"The kitchen, madame."

"The kitchen?" Her tone was full of disapproval. She marched on.

"I thought it best to fetch you, monsieur," the servant said. "This man is not alone, and I do not want to alarm the Vicomtesse de Merville."

"Who is with him?" Hugh asked.

"I…would rather not say, monsieur. Blakeney asked for the comtesse. She did not answer her door and…"

"I see." So Blakeney had arrived with a friend and wanted Angelette. Hugh couldn't begin to make sense of it all until he stepped into the kitchen. Then everything became clear.

A man in a French army uniform, bloodied and torn, sat at a table where the chef tended his wounds. His face was badly bruised and blood had dried and caked in his light hair. He was perhaps forty, and his hair was a mixture of blond and gray. Angelette stopped short when she saw him, and Hugh had to bank hard to the right to avoid running into her. Sir Percy stood off to one side, his gaze on Angelette and then Hugh. Hugh shook his head, anger welling inside him. The man's uniform gave all away, and yet Hugh hoped he was mistaken.

"You take an enormous risk bringing him here," Hugh said.

Angelette turned to Hugh. "I don't understand. Who is he?"

The man raised his head. "I am Victor Eugène, Baron dc Luberon."

Hugh kept his gaze on Blakeney. "Tell us the rest, Sir Percy."

Blakeney inclined his head. "The baron is the second-in-command at the Bastille."

Angelette raised her hands to her face. "Are you seriously injured, monsieur?" She moved closer to the baron, kneeling before him.

"No, madame. The people wanted my superior, the marquis. I was beaten and kicked aside."

"But now the leaders of the uprising have realized the baron is not among those they took prisoner," Sir Percy said. "They are searching for him and, make no mistake, if he is found, he will be killed."

"Then he must not go home," Angelette said.

"He can't stay here," Hugh interjected. Angelette had not yet realized that was Sir Percy's plan.

She spun around. "But he has nowhere else to go. We can't send him away."

"That is not your decision to make. This is not our house."

"Then I suppose it is my decision."

They all turned to find the Vicomte de Merville standing in the doorway. He was dressed as he had been earlier and had obviously not yet gone to bed.

"I heard the commotion and came down." He addressed himself to the baron. "Monsieur, you are welcome here as long as you like. I only wish I could do more to help you, but my wife is with child and we must leave as soon as possible." He glanced at Sir Percy.

"Have no fear, monsieur. I will return in a few hours with the coaches I promised. Only I will not be traveling with you."

"But Sir Percy, it is too dangerous to stay," Hugh argued. If Sir Percy stayed, what hope did he have of convincing Angelette to go?

"It is far more dangerous for the baron," Sir Percy argued, "and he will not be able to escape the city without papers. I will give him mine and stay behind until I am able to acquire replacements."

The baron stood, his hand on the table to steady himself. "I cannot ask such a thing of you, monsieur."

Sir Percy waved a hand, and Hugh noted that under his military-style coat, he wore a shirt with lace cuffs. "It is already decided. I will hear no argument. Furthermore, if I stay there may be others I can help as well."

"Then you must use this residence as a place of safety. The vicomtesse and I will be gone. I would like to think of this home as a place of refuge for those in need."

Sir Percy bowed deeply. "I am very much obliged to you, monsieur."

"Apparently, no one considers the danger Sir Percy puts the four of us in when he adds the baron to our traveling party. What if the guards at the gate or the customs officials discover the baron's true identity? We could all be imprisoned. Or worse."

"This gentleman is correct," the baron said. "I cannot allow you to risk your lives for mine."

"I can think of no greater honor," the vicomte replied. "You are welcome to travel in my coach."

All eyes turned to Hugh. With a sigh he looked at Angelette. "Will you reconsider if we take the baron with us? Will you come to England?"

Angelette looked at the baron and then at Hugh. "I'm afraid I've answered this question already. I will not be traveling to England in the morning."

# Twelve

Hugh grasped her shoulders. "What the devil do you mean? You were at the Bastille. You saw the mobs with the severed heads. Of course, you are coming to London."

She had known this would be the most difficult aspect of her decision. She did not want to leave Hugh, but she knew what she must do. "I am not. I will stay in France."

"Angelette." His face was a storm of anger and worry. "We have been through this. It is too dangerous. Your life could be—no, *will* be in danger. These people who attacked the Bastille today want all tyranny eradicated. The king is weak and indecisive. The longer he dithers, the stronger they will grow. Today they came for the Bastille. Next they may come for the nobility or the priests. They have already burnt down your home. What more proof do you need that if you stay you risk your life?"

"It is a risk I am willing to take." She reached up and placed her hands over his on her shoulders. Her own hands were cold against his, but hers were steady. She had made up her mind. She took his hand and pulled him aside, desperate to speak to him in private. The others turned away, giving them a semblance of privacy. "Please believe I want to go with you." She looked up into his eyes, and she saw the hurt. "I love you. I don't know how it happened or when. I know we met only days ago, but I feel as though I have known you my whole life. I love you, Hugh, but I cannot go with you to England. My work is here. I've felt that all along, and I wish I could pretend it was not so and run away with you. But I cannot. People here need my help. Sir Percy and I can work together and help far more than either of us ever could alone."

Hugh clasped her hand tightly. "Don't do this. We can have a life in England."

"I hope we may someday. But right now my life is here." It pained her, but she pulled her hand away. "I must dress. Sir Percy and I must make plans."

She felt Hugh's gaze burn the skin of her back as she walked away.

Angelette did not see Hugh the rest of the night. She assumed he slept. He had almost nothing to pack for the journey in the morning. She had not wanted their last night to end as it had. She had planned to tell him in the morning that she had not changed her mind and could not travel with him. The arrival of the baron had ruined her plans, but she could not fault Sir Percy. She could only pray he and the rest of the group would arrive safely in England.

In the kitchen, she sipped coffee alone. She was not tired, and if she had tried to sleep, she would have only been kept awake by worry that the *vainqueurs* would discover where the baron had fled, knock on the door, and demand she deliver the baron to them. And so she was still awake at daybreak when Sir Percy arrived with the coaches. He brought the conveyances into the small yard in the back rather than leaving them on the Rue Saint-Honoré, as was customary. But the de Mervilles did not wish for attention surrounding their departure.

While the coachmen saw to the horses, Angelette beckoned Sir Percy inside. "Coffee, Sir Percy?"

"Sink me, no." He wore a blue morning coat with blue breeches and a yellow waistcoat embroidered with the red pimpernel flowers he seemed to so enjoy. His hair was pulled back into a queue and not powdered, but he looked freshly pressed and rested, though she was certain he hadn't slept any more than she.

"You are earlier than expected."

"Better to be early than late, I always say. The vicomte and Lord Daventry will be ready soon enough."

"May I speak with you, Sir Percy?" she asked, gesturing toward the table. He raised a brow, but sat opposite her, seeming unsurprised by the gesture.

"You want to tell me you are not leaving for London. Eaves-dropping is very bad form, but I'm afraid I could not help overhearing."

"That is part of it," she acknowledged, seating herself across from him. "I am staying in Paris—in this house—and I hope you will allow me to help you with your work."

"Your aid would be much appreciated, madame. As a foreigner, my neighbors take note of my comings and goings. That is why I did not bring the baron to my lodgings. This house is a godsend." His tone had grown quite serious now. "And, forgive me if this is too bold, I understand your late husband was quite wealthy. Forged papers are not inexpensive."

Angelette nodded. "I understand and when the uproar in the city dies down I will see my solicitor and obtain funds for our cause. I only wish I could do more. Lord Daventry imports wine and has contacts all over the countryside. I had hoped I might persuade him to help."

"He may yet change his mind."

Angelette smiled, but she felt no hope. "Until that time," she said, "we will need allies. English allies."

"I know several men in my club who have been waiting for the right time to act."

"I would say that time is now. When you are able to get papers, I would like you to travel to London and approach these men, ask them to form a…a league of sorts."

He nodded. "Many will flee France as a result of the riots yesterday. I heard the king's brothers plan to depart as soon as possible. But many others will stay and will need help in the future."

"It must be a secret league," she said. "No one in France or England must know who ranks among the members."

"Or the identity of our leader." He nodded at her, and she felt her cheeks heat.

"I am not the leader."

"I beg to differ, but I think it best to protect you. If I go to London to recruit the members of our league, then it will be assumed I am the de facto leader. If at some point our league is discovered and I am sought or taken, you will still be free to continue our operations."

"I agree secrecy is of the utmost importance. Cleverness as well. We must find masters of disguise and forgery. Men and women who are not afraid to risk everything to save the lives of the innocent."

Sir Percy tapped a finger on his jaw. "We need a name, I think. The League to Save France?"

Angelette wrinkled her nose. "I thought the idea was not to be discovered. The name must not reveal who we are. How about the League..." She looked about for some sort of inspiration, and her gaze landed on his waistcoat. "The League of the Pimpernel. No, the Scarlet Pimpernel."

He smiled. "That's perfect! I only wish I could begin recruiting members now."

"Perhaps you can," Hugh said. He stepped into the doorway, and Angelette started with surprise.

"How long have you been there?" she asked. Had he heard all of their plan? She would have to be more careful in the future. And now she would have to change the name of their league. It wasn't that she did not trust Hugh, but he was not one of them.

"Long enough to know that you need me."

She shook her head. "I don't understand."

Hugh gestured to Sir Percy. "Clearly Blakeney needs to travel to London as soon as possible. In order to do so, he will need his papers. I propose Sir Percy depart with the baron and the de Mervilles and the baron use my papers to escape to London."

"My lord, you understand that would leave you trapped in Paris." Sir Percy rose.

Hugh's gaze met Angelette's. "I understand."

"I don't know that's wise," Sir Percy said. "I have contacts and know forgers. I can get new papers relatively quickly. It may take weeks for me to return and procure papers for you."

Hugh shrugged, his gaze never leaving Angelette. "Then I wait weeks."

"And what will you do if the people form mobs as they did before? They may begin murdering the nobility."

"I'm not wholly without resources," Hugh said. "As Angelette has mentioned, I know wine merchants all over the countryside. Most are loyal to me and would hide me or friends of mine if need be. Not to mention, wine barrels would make an excellent tool for slipping people out of the city."

"You would help me?" Angelette gestured to Sir Percy. "Help us, I should say."

"I too have funds," Hugh went on. "And ships. It might be useful to have our own ships rather than relying on French captains."

"That is all very true, and I would be glad to have you," Sir Percy said. "But you did not answer the comtesse's question."

Hugh looked at her again. "You asked if I would help you."

She nodded.

"The answer depends."

"On?"

"On your answer." He sank to one knee, and she inhaled sharply. "Angelette, will you marry me?"

"You can't mean that," she sputtered. "I've been nothing but trouble. You want to return to England. You cannot wish to tie yourself to me and Paris."

"I do want to return to England, but I realized something else over the past few hours—I want to be wherever you are. London. Paris. Hell."

She smiled, tears blurring her vision.

"I will follow you anywhere. You've utterly ruined me for any other woman."

"I don't know what to say," she whispered, her voice failing her.

"Say yes!" Sir Percy all but shouted.

She laughed. "Yes!"

Hugh rose and took her into his arms. He held her tightly, then lowered his mouth to kiss her. She had intended only to kiss him back briefly, but once their lips met she couldn't seem to let go. After a moment she heard Sir Percy clear his throat. "I had better return to my lodgings and gather what I need. Tell the de Mervilles—never mind. I shall tell them myself."

Hugh pulled back and held her face in his hands. "I cannot believe you said yes."

"I cannot believe you are staying."

"I could never leave you, even if it means I must join the League of the Scarlet Pimpernel, which, by the way, needs a better name."

"The League of the Yellow Daisy?"

"I was thinking something that doesn't reference flowers."

"Really? I rather like it."

He sighed. "You are in charge."

"That's right. I am." And she kissed him again.

# *Thirteen*

Thomas wrinkled his brow and sat back in the chair across from his father. At some point during the tale, Thomas had poured himself a drink, but he hadn't consumed much—except when his father went on about how beautiful his mother had been or that sappy story of how he'd proposed marriage. He'd needed a large swallow then.

"I don't think I quite understand," Thomas said. "You knew Sir Percy, and he began the League of the Scarlet Pimpernel, but he was not the person in charge of the league."

His father removed his spectacles and rubbed the bridge of his nose. He looked almost like a man emerging from a dream. "That's correct. He took the credit and the fall, when necessary, but in truth, he was only one of the members of the league. Granted, he was quite important. As was Ffoulkes, of course."

"Then were you the Scarlet Pimpernel?" Thomas asked. "You seemed to be saying...that is, in the story it sounded as though..."

"As though your mother was the Scarlet Pimpernel?"

Thomas couldn't even manage to nod.

"I'd say that was correct. Wouldn't you agree, *mon ange*?"

Thomas jumped to his feet as his mother moved across the room. He wasn't certain when she'd entered the library. He certainly hadn't heard the door open or her skirts rustle. She stopped to give Thomas a kiss on the cheek, smelling of apples and the countryside as she always had. Her dark hair had a bit of gray in it now and a few wrinkles appeared at the creases of her eyes and mouth. She was almost always smiling. The viscountess looked up at him. "How lovely of you to visit, Thomas. You're not in some sort of trouble, are you?"

Thomas sighed. "Why does everyone assume I am in trouble? I only wished to speak with Father."

She turned to smile at her husband. "About the Scarlet Pimpernel of all things? That's ancient history."

"Then why do I feel like I don't know the whole story?"

"I never knew you cared." She moved around the desk where his father stood and motioned for him to sit. Then she situated herself on the arm of his chair. "You were always much keener to talk of horses than history. In fact, we once had a letter from Eton where the dean despaired—"

"I'm interested now, Mother," Thomas said with no little exasperation. "Father claims you were the Scarlet Pimpernel. Is he trying to bamboozle me?"

"No," she said. "It's true, though I certainly didn't work alone. In a sense no one person was the Scarlet Pimpernel. We all were. But I suppose I founded the league, along with your father and Sir Percy. And, of course, I devised the moniker, though Sir Percy is largely to thank for that as well."

Thomas stared at his mother. She had always been happy to stay at home and play or read to Thomas and his sisters. The most adventurous thing he'd ever seen her do was go for a picnic when the skies looked like rain. And she was a woman! Women did not rescue prisoners from the blade of the guillotine or sneak them out of Paris in the dead of night. How could his mother, the woman who had tucked him in at night and fretted because he didn't wear mittens in cold weather, possibly be the Scarlet Pimpernel?

Thomas straightened his coat. "I think I had better return to Town."

His mother stood. "You won't stay to dinner? Your sisters will be so disappointed."

He had intended to stay to dinner, but now he had no appetite. His mother...?

Thomas shook his head. "I had better start back."

"Well, at least ask Cook to send some food along with you. We can go to the kitchens and pack something for the journey."

His father wrapped an arm about her waist. "In a moment."

She gave the viscount an indulgent smile. "Very well." She looked at Thomas again. "I will meet you in the kitchen shortly."

He nodded. "Thank you, Mother. And, thank you for the...story, Father."

"Come and visit again soon," his father said.

"And next time stay to dinner and to see your sisters," his mother added.

Thomas went to the door and stepped outside. As he closed the door behind him, he stole a look into the library. His father had pulled his mother onto his lap, and she was laughing, her arms about his neck.

"I don't think he believed me," his father was saying.

"Sometimes I hardly believe it myself. We were young and reckless."

"*You* were reckless. I wanted to keep you alive so I could bring you back to England with me."

"And in the end you had your way."

Thomas leaned a shoulder against the door's casement. He'd always found the affection between his parents vaguely nauseating. He didn't mind it so much today. In fact, he rather envied it.

"Do you regret it?" his mother was asking. "The years in Paris, the constant danger, the hours spent hiding and plotting and running?"

"Not a single minute. You?"

She shook her head. "I remember the looks of gratitude on the faces of those we saved. I'd do it all over again."

"And that, *mon ange,* is why I love you."

Her answer was a kiss.

Thomas moved away from the door then. He'd return to London and find Ffoulkes. Surely there must be other untold stories of the Scarlet Pimpernel. Perhaps poetry was not his calling. He'd always wanted to write a work of fiction...

He heard his mother laugh again, and Thomas paused just before a painting of his mother that hung in an all-but-forgotten alcove. She was young in the painting, seated outdoors in a country setting under a large tree. Her cheeks were pink, as was her dress, and she'd been picking flowers. On her arm rested a woven basket overflowing with flowers. Red flowers...

Thomas didn't have to open a book on botany to know what he would learn. How had he never seen it before? Those flowers were, quite obviously, scarlet pimpernels. What else had he missed? What other secrets hid in plain sight? He looked back at his father's library. Unplumbed depths indeed. He'd have to come home more often.

# Want to read more in the Scarlet Chronicles series?

The next book in the series, *Traitor in Her Arms*, is available now! And here's a sneak peek at *Taken by the Rake,* available February 12, 2019!

Paris terrified her. The daily executions, the violence in the streets, the National Guard, who ransacked houses nightly in search of royalist sympathizers. Honoria Blake *hated* Paris.

And yet, she couldn't seem to make herself leave.

She had no one but herself to blame for the fact that she wasn't tucked in safe under the roof of her flat in London. No one but herself to blame that she was stuffing feathers back into a mattress that had been bayoneted and all but destroyed by the Guard not once but three times in the past month she'd been here. No one to blame but herself that she was tired and on edge.

No but herself and, perhaps in part, Monsieur Palomer.

Hiding three men of the League of the Scarlet Pimpernel under the floorboards in her bedchamber for half the night could have that effect on a person. Especially when Lord Anthony Dewhurst, Lord Edward Hastings, and Sir Andrew Ffoulkes were among Robespierre and his Committee of Public Safety's most wanted.

No one suspected two women—herself and Alexandra Martin—of being in league with the Pimpernel. The soldiers searched the safe house—could she call it a safe house when it had been searched three times in thirty days?— never pausing to consider that two members of the league they sought stood directly before them.

Honoria could not have said precisely what Alexandra did for the Pimpernel. She suspected Alex ferried aristos through Paris and into the countryside so they could be taken to safety in England. Alex was also in charge of disguises, and she had a remarkable talent there. She could make a large, dark man like Dewhurst look old and decrepit. She could make the burly Scot Mackenzie look like a woman—not an attractive woman but not an ugly one either. And when Alex wasn't leading aristos through the catacombs running under the city of Paris, she was performing on the stage. She had a small part in a production of *Le Jugement dernier des roi* at The People's Theater.

Honoria sneezed as she stuffed the last feather into the mattress. It had taken all morning but the room was finally put to rights. She didn't even want to think about the mess awaiting her in the drawing room. Thank God all the papers and correspondence the League needed were hidden in a false panel in the dining room wall. Not only would it have doomed them if the soldiers had discovered the documents, she would be the one cleaning up the shredded foolscap before she, too, was dragged to prison.

Honoria's work for the Pimpernel was neither as exciting nor as dangerous as that of the others. Her skills were in forgery and document creation. She could sign Robespierre's name better than he could, and the papers she made for the aristos escaping Paris looked as authentic as any issued by the Committee for Public Safety. She could duplicate the stamp, the embossing, and every other minute detail.

The nature of her work meant she rarely left the safe house. For the most part, she did not mind. The safe house was, as the name would suggest, relatively safe. But in the back of her mind one small point niggled. She hadn't begged the Pimpernel to bring her to Paris so she could be safe. She would have been safe in her little room in the back of Montagu House. She could have continued making false passports for him there.

But Honoria had wanted adventure. She'd wanted to make a difference. She'd wanted to experience life. She'd been hiding from the age of fifteen. Now, at the age of six and twenty, she wasn't afraid any longer. But she was still hiding behind severe hairstyles, drab shapeless dresses, and enormous glasses she did not need. Even with all of that, Dewhurst had described her as "too demmed pretty to go out alone," and Ffoulkes had said she might go out at night but "in the daylight you'd draw too much attention."

Alex had worked her magic, making Honoria look sallow and pock-marked with missing teeth. She'd been able to go out then, but she'd been terrified someone might discover her disguise and begin asking questions.

And so she stayed inside and hid herself away. She'd probably go home to London in a few days. What would she have to show for her efforts? Ink stains on her fingers and bags under her eyes. How was that any different from London? She'd been forging passports and papers to France for the last few years. Not on a daily or even a weekly basis, but a couple one month and a few more several months later. And then Monsieur Palomer had walked into her cramped chamber at the British Museum. She hadn't wanted to hear his tales of the horrors in Paris. She'd read of them in the papers and that had been enough. But she hadn't been able to make him stop talking, and something about listening to him recount what he'd seen was so much worse than merely reading about it.

His eyes had been haunted. He didn't want to go back to France, but he felt he must. He had family and friends trapped in Paris, and he could not leave them to their fate. He wasn't a noble but a drapery merchant to the nobility. His curtains had hung at Versailles. His factory had been burned and looted, many of his workers killed, and his family threatened. He'd been in England for business and was afraid to go back using his real name. He wanted to save his family and as many others as he could.

Honoria had made him the necessary papers and watched him walk out the door. She'd never seen or heard of him again, and she had looked for mentions of him or his family.

Had he died? Had he lived? Had he saved his family?

Did anyone care about all the innocent people trapped in the senseless violence of Paris? And if she did, what was she doing about it?

The next time an émigré had come to her with a request for false papers she'd made it known she wanted to work for the Scarlet Pimpernel. She didn't even know if he was real, but if she was to go to France and help, she knew he was her best hope.

It hadn't taken long for the Pimpernel to find her.

"Miss Blake!"

Honoria wiped her brow and rose to go to the door of the tiny room she shared with Alex. That had to be Dewhurst yelling. He would have bellowed prayers in church, and despite the fact that he was one of the sons of the Duke of Exeter, he had the worst manners of the lot of them.

"Yes?" She added, *my lord* mentally because even though they had no servants in the house and never any guests, they were careful as to how they addressed each other. They had false names, of course. French names, but though Ffoulkes was always reminding them to use the false names at all times, they rarely did when at home alone.

"We are for the market. A little shopping."

She no longer believed they were actually going to the market. The first few times she'd been told this, she'd asked after their missing packages when they'd returned. Now she understood *shopping* meant a mission. She moved to the landing at the top of the stairs so she could see Dewhurst. He stood at the bottom dressed in the rough clothes of a revolutionary complete with a carmagnole jacket and a Phrygian cap on his inky black hair. He'd wound a red and white striped sash about his waist, where the handle of a pistol peeked out. His face had a light layer of dirt and grime on it, and if he looked a little too healthy, too well-fed to have stepped out of the Faubourg Saint-Antoine, no one would question him too closely. The dangerous glint in his eye tended to discourage questions.

That and the bloody pike he liked to carry.

"I do hope you find a bargain," she answered. It was the accepted way for her to wish them good luck.

"Lock the doors and stay inside."

"I will." She kept her gaze on his face and not on the pike.

"Work in the dining room with the panel open. If anyone comes to the door—"

"I *know* what to do."

"If he is one of ours, he'll know the signal or have the mark." Dewhurst narrowed his eyes, waiting until she nodded. "Even then, be careful."

"Of course." She'd heard it all so many times, but she didn't blame him for reminding her. The Pimpernel himself might be in Paris right now. If he came to the door, she wouldn't know him. She'd corresponded with him, even spoken to him on half a dozen occasions but she'd never seen his face, and the few times she'd caught a glimpse of him, he'd been in disguise.

"What if something goes wrong?" she asked.

Dewhurst had been about to turn and walk away, but now he paused and gave her a long look. He had dark eyes, and they looked even darker in the enclosed space of the stairwell.

"It won't. *Au revoir.*"

*"Au revoir. Bon chance."*

She heard a rumble of voices, the sound of the door, and then she was alone. Left behind, as usual.

She started back up the steps and made the mistake of peeking into the drawing room.

Left behind to clean up the mess. With a sigh, she bent to pick up a fallen pillow.

\*\*\*

Laurent looked up through a haze of sweat and blood and into the face of the devil. The devil was not a horned red creature with a forked tail, as the painters made him out to be. Neither was he the golden angel fallen from heaven. The devil was the frenzied mob butchering the helpless inmates of La Force.

The devil was the peasants of France.

He'd closed his eyes then, giving in to the peace that would come with death. If hell had come to earth, certainly death could be no worse. The shrieks and groans faded away, and he felt only the warmth of the sun and the cool of the breeze on his face.

"Citoyen Bourgogne."

Something sharp prodded his ribs.

"Open your eyes. Citoyen, wake up."

"He's dead. Leave him."

The voices crashed over him, rousing him from the only peace he'd known in months.

"He's awake."

Laurent opened his eyes and scowled at the men looking down at him. One glance beyond them told him he was no longer in the prison courtyard. Where was he? Where was the mob? Perhaps this was the mob. Perhaps they'd saved him for last.

"Well," he rasped. "Go ahead and kill me."

"It's tempting," said a tall man with dark hair, who was dressed in the revolutionary garb of sans coulottes and carmagnole. He was larger and healthier than most peasants.

His shoulders strained his dingy brown shirt, hinting at muscles and power beneath. His size and strength meant he wielded more authority. That and he had a pistol. At one time in his life, Laurent would have given his right hand for a pistol.

Laurent stared at the pistol. "Can you shoot straight, citoyen?"

"As an arrow," the man answered, his accent not that of the poorer faubourgs like Saint-Antoine but not that of Versailles either.

Laurent squared his shoulders. "Then do it. Right between the eyes or through the heart is preferred, though I doubt you care for my wishes."

"Not particularly, no. You deserved to die at the hands of those lunatics, but I saved you."

"For the guillotine?" Laurent asked. It was a stupid question, but clearly some peasant had damaged his head. Laurent's temple throbbed, and he had a vague memory of a wooden axe handle coming down on him. He'd lost too much blood. Why else would he believe this revolutionary had come to save him?

"I saved you for *him*." The man grabbed Laurent's hand and pressed what felt like foolscap into it. "Now stand."

He roughly yanked Laurent to his knees. The world rushed at him, green and brown and red, but he managed to stay on his feet. He was no longer inside the gates of La Force. He was free and weaving along an alley. If the muted sounds of violence in the distance were any indication, he was not far from La Force and the mob carnage being wrought there.

At the end of the alleyway, the big revolutionary pushed Laurent toward two men standing at the corner of the courtyard wall. One had auburn hair peeking out from under a rag on his head and the other blond hair under a cocked hat. Three men. Laurent thought he might have a chance to escape them…except for that pistol.

Just then a fourth man ran full tilt from the adjoining street. He was dressed in sans coulottes and carmagnole like the first. "Lads! This wye. We hae a problem."

Laurent couldn't place the accent at first—French tinged with Scottish? A Scot?

"You too!" The Scot pointed to the revolutionary pushing Laurent. "Leave him."

"Bloody hell," the revolutionary growled in English. Then he reached into his blood-stained vest and pulled out a slip of paper. "This is a house where you'll be safe," he said in French. "Go now, but stay off the main avenues."

Laurent took the paper. "And if I don't go to this house?"

The revolutionary gave him a hard look before running after his compatriots. "Then don't expect to survive until tomorrow," he called over his shoulder.

And he was gone.

Laurent leaned against the wall of the alley, his head throbbing even worse now, and opened the paper.

*6 Rue du Jour*

Laurent did not move. One moment he had been inside the prison courtyard, fighting the mob climbing over the walls and crashing through what should have been a locked gate. The next moment he was free and being told to go to a house on the Rue du Jour.

He had the urge to return to the prison. Perhaps he could save some of the women and children, and when he died, take a few of the revolutionaries with him. But he remembered the last images of the courtyard before he'd closed his eyes. He'd watched as two women tore at the dress and hair of Camille. She was covered in blood, and he'd hoped she was no longer alive. Once, in another life, when he'd been the Marquis de Montagne and she the Vicomtesse de la Chapelle they'd danced in the gardens of

Versailles and sipped champagne. He'd kissed her once, her lips as sweet with the wine as the strings of the violins.

There was no sweetness in France any longer.

It was too late to save the prisoners who'd been in the courtyard.

Laurent had a choice. He could lie down here and die or he could try to make it to 6 Rue du Jour. Whatever lay in store for him there, he did not think it was death.

Laurent stumbled out of the alleyway and tried to orient himself. It took a few minutes before he knew where he was and could start off in the right direction. He passed men and women hurrying along the streets. Most looked at him then looked away. They knew what was happening in the prison of La Force, but they'd do nothing to stop it.

Oh, the good people of Paris.

Laurent continued on, stumbling through the narrow streets, keeping his head down, ignoring the drops of scarlet that fell from his temple. He almost ran into the man who stepped in front of him, blocking his path. Laurent fell back as the man hefted a cudgel. "And what do we have here?"

The man was a revolutionary from the tricolor cockade he wore to his striped culottes. It would have been easy enough to stay down, to close his eyes, and allow this peasant to do his worst. But now that his head was clear, he remembered he couldn't die. He had made a promise, and he had to live to fulfill it.

Laurent climbed back to his feet. "Get out of my way."

"A noble," the man said with a grin. "I've just come from La Force, and I'll wager you did too."

"I don't know what you're talking about. I'm on my way home."

"You are on your way to the devil. *Mort à l'aristocratie!*" the man screamed. His face, already marred with blood and dirt from the sweat of his labors, turned red. He raised his cudgel with a malevolent grin, showing his broken teeth.

This was not the way Laurent had thought he would die. He'd imagined he'd die from a drunken tumble into the Seine or from a wild horseback ride or falling out of the gondola of a *globe aérostatique* all his friends had been so keen to try. Death during a balloon flight would have been far more romantic than death from bludgeoning at the hands of a peasant with no care for dental hygiene.

Laurent simply couldn't allow it. The peasant swung the cudgel, and Laurent caught the man's wrist, stopping the weapon's progress. The peasant's eyes widened, and Laurent squeezed his wrist until he heard the bones crunch. With a cry, the man released the weapon, and it fell to the ground with a clink. But Laurent's victory was short-lived. Windows opened and a woman screamed for the guard.

Laurent was no match for armed soldiers, and he began to run. He ran without looking where he was going, and by the time he realized he had outpaced the peasants, he was lost. He was thirsty and hot, yet shivering uncontrollably. He knew Paris as he knew the body of a lover, but when he looked about now, he had no idea where he was.

And then his eyes locked on the sign.

*Rue du Jour.*

Somehow, even in the chaos, his feet had known which path to take. Staggering with weariness, Laurent pushed himself toward the house at number six.

*Pre-order now!*

# About Shana Galen

Shana Galen is three-time Rita award nominee and the bestselling author of passionate Regency romps. "The road to happily-ever-after is intense, conflicted, suspenseful and fun," and *RT Bookreviews* calls her books "lighthearted yet poignant, humorous yet touching." She taught English at the middle and high school level off and on for eleven years. Most of those years were spent working in Houston's inner city. Now she writes full time, surrounded by three cats and one spoiled dog. She's happily married and has a daughter who is most definitely a romance heroine in the making.

Would you like exclusive content, book news, and a chance to win early copies of Shana's books? Sign up for monthly emails for exclusive news and giveaways on Shana's website, www.shanagalen.com.

Made in the USA
San Bernardino, CA
24 January 2019